**YELLOW SIGNS ARE SUGGESTIONS
WHITE SIGNS ARE RULES MASQUERADING AS LAWS
TRUE LAWS CANNOT BE BROKEN
...IT'S HARD TO TELL THE DIFFERENCE**

"There is indeed a magic in these pages...it's always provocative, strangely compelling and not easily forgotten. A story that is different each time you read it."

—Teresa Kennedy(TED Staff editor)

"I found myself falling in love with the book. The novel is rich in its meditation upon the human existence and complex in its existentialism. A skillful job of blending traditional story elements with a philosophical exploration. I am proud to add this book on my prized shelf of personalized copies."

—Andrew Meisenheimer
(Acquisition Editor for Zondervon, a Harper Collins company)

"An Intense Love Story." —from the PPCC book club

ROAD SIGNS

Jay Archer David

Natural Selection LLC

Publishing

Road Signs

by Jay Archer David

www.road-signs.org

Copyright © 2010 by Jay Archer David

Published by Natural Selection LLC

International Standard Book Number:978-0-9828978-0-5

Library of Congress Control Number: 2010933740

Printed in the United States of America

Cover photography by J. McCampbell S. (jes@naturalselection-llc.com)

Cover design by Kirk DouPonce, cover concept Alex Vertikoff

To Joanie,

Angel, compass, wife —
We entered this life within
hours of each other,
We share it,
Love,
Endure, and
Teach each other...

And knew from the start
That we would only leave
together!

A C K N O W L E D G M E N T S

I appreciate all who arrived to become connected to this work. Apart from being an extremely gifted editor, Andrew Meisenheimer is a fellow creator. Andy always seems to know when there is much more, just under the surface, waiting to burst forth, and with a skillful, light touch, he gently coaxes it out. Kirk DouPonce's artistry has put the face on this novel. He remained cheerful and inspired throughout the many revisions as we worked to get just the right feel. A special thanks to Ross Browne and his crew at The Editorial Department. In my humble opinion, they are where editing and publishing support is going. Finally, what would I have done without my first readers including my wife, my mother, Mary Carrol Nelson, and Alex Vertikoff? Their reactions to Road Signs paved the way.

The future influences the present just as much as the past

- Nietzsche

ROAD SIGNS

POST-GENESIS

¹ And on the afternoon of the eighth day, God checked back to see what had occurred.

² Upon looking down, God saw that man had created Road in man's own image.

³ And the Road was good!

⁴ And on the Road arose one-point-two Autos for every driver.

⁵ The Road, along with the Autos, gathered together unto one place all that man was: The light and the darkness of man, the heavens and the earth in man, the creeping things of man that creepeth, and the flying things of man that soareth. And behold, it was very good.

⁶ Thus the Road and the Autos were completed and all the host of them. Only they had to be constantly re-created, for the Road continued to need widening, and the autos kept breaking down.

⁷ So man never rested from all his work that he had made.

8 Man traveled the Road for his pride and pleasure, and also his grief.

9 Man learned and grew from the Road, but also grew in dependency upon it.

10 So, on the evening of the eighth day, God, being in experimental muse, made vanish from the earth all the Road that was between places,

. . . to see what man would do.

Long Road Home

Even now, driving home in this lazy line of sunburned vehicles, my body remembered *the rock*, the unbelievably blunt impact of nearly a ton of boulder that shouldn't have moved, hadn't moved in centuries—but I had set it loose.

I wanted to stop the scene from replaying in my mind but couldn't. I had left something a hundred miles back in that high cleft, something aside from a lifeless crag, fragments of a torn garment, and tissue ripped from my body by vertical walls of jagged sandstone.

All I knew was that I should return home now. Further, I should want to—or need to. Why was it so hard?

Out my driver's-side window an impossible rock formation swept into view. I turned my head slightly left to better see it, glad for the distraction. A chiseled and eroding mesa sprang from the red desert's low rolling hills. Towering atop the mesa's spine was an enormous flat boulder precariously balanced on a stubby pillar. The boulder's topside was awash in brilliant sunlight, while its underbelly was in perpetual shadow. By every law, the monolith should fall, but there it stood, obstinately perched in spite of natural forces chipping at its knobby pedestal. I wondered vaguely who might be around for its eventual downfall, who would mourn.

As I stared at the geological oddity, a bright yellow sign flew past, warning of a sharp curve ahead and displaying text that read "35 mph."

I ignored it.

Yellow signs are suggestions.

Instead I watched the balanced rock fade from my driver's -side mirror. As it bid farewell, I saw another vehicle slow to join the rear of our small line of traffic.

The cause for the jam-up in the otherwise empty desert was a leisurely rig crawling on the highway 10 yards in front of my bumper. It was natural to blame the plodding RV for my lack of progress. After all, it was a difficult thing to get around.

The backside of this slow-moving camper was fast becoming the symbol of unseen forces keeping me from home. It lumbered around twists and turns in an arid landscape, blocking everything else from view until I was blind except for the sight of it.

The vehicle's chrome bumper flashed with reflected sun, creating dazzling spots of light that bounced merrily on the asphalt road. The light was inviting me. I looked away. But a rhythm slowly ca-chunked from its suspension as its frame gracefully rose and fell like a ship on a gentle sea. My eyes grew affixed yet again. Its yellow paint was cheerful, its smooth lines peaceful, its timeless pace that of Kairos.

It truly irritated me.

Suddenly I couldn't stand it, not for a moment more. Accelerating to close the gap between us, I started searching for any opportunity to pass.

None came.

Minutes turned into miles.

Irritation became annoyance and I began to regard the driver's languid pace as a personal affront.

After an interminable span of time I finally muttered, "This guy's an idiot!"

Now there are at least a hundred expletives I could have chosen to describe and otherwise nail this fellow interfering with my space on the road. All motorists know how to utter these loudly from the safe confines of their glassed-in environment. Some motorists still dare Italian moments wherein they enhance these descriptions with hand gestures. However, with the advent of road rage and the uncertainty of the seat-side weaponry that might accompany the offending driver, more and more hands stay on the wheel, and insults are shouted without moving the lips.

For those of us who are mild of manner, outbursts might include "Will you look at this guy? and "Jeez, what a jerk." For the normal of manner, descriptions venture quickly to the profane. But regardless of all the dizzying, creative ways to peg them, bad drivers generally fall into just two categories. Those who drive poorly and shouldn't be on the road are *idiots*. Those who drive rudely or recklessly, heedless to how vulnerable 90-mile-an-hour flesh is to tortured metal and glass, who would risk your life whilst being cavalier with their own—those are *assholes*.

And this guy going a few miles an hour under the speed limit on a winding two-lane highway with eight cars lined up behind him needing to pass—this guy was an idiot.

Oblivious to patterns imprinted on me by countless years of road conditioning, I summarily judged the slow driver and condemned him. I had never paused to consider this kind of response before. I was sure my assessment of him would be confirmed if ever I met him at a rest stop or a gas station, but I wasn't about to slow down enough to meet this poke-along, not anywhere. He would soon be no more than a glimpse in my rearview mirror.

Or so I thought. Today would be different; just a little twist, something under the surface was jolting me. It had been the same last night when I'd spent hours sleepless in a sleeping bag, haunted, reliving *the rock* over and over.

Outside my driver's window, the sunbathed road and peaceful arid landscape ceased to be, and in their place was that scene of panic that looped endlessly in every one of my nerve bundles, every memory of muscle fiber.

Amid the rush of adrenaline, my nervous system had signaled *put out arms*, and my arms sprang upward. With lightning reflexes, my hands flattened against the cold, massive, and moving stone. In that same instant came the thought: Hold the boulder there, above and in front of me, or delay it just long enough to nimbly escape upward, up and around.

No problem; no chance. In slow motion, it came down with dreadful energy. I had set it free. Nothing would stop it, nothing could stop it, and I was squarely in its path.

In that moment *What?* turned into *NO!*

Pride goeth, and then pain, pain like I'd never experienced.

"Internal damage!" I remember hearing my voice report aloud to no one in particular as my belly button smashed into my spine. Then as I crumpled, new signals arrived. It was fresh agony from my right arm, which had been used as indifferently as a rail under the brutish weight of sledding Moenkopi sandstone. I held the flopping arm feebly. There was nothing to do but experience the pyrotechnics of exploding nerves.

In all the years before now, I had never been really hurt. That changed in a millisecond. Behind tears, waves of agony, and closed eyes, my mind retraced all the chimneys and wall scrambling I had done to get up into this chute. How would I ever climb back down to humanity?

I eased off the gas and stopped pushing on that invisible comfort zone between the idiot's rear bumper and my front one. At some level I decided not to bolt around him.

I'll go his speed.

As I opened a gap between our bumpers, a slick, bright red Mustang swung out from behind me, darted into the hole I'd just made, and then out again into oncoming traffic. He was taking this opportunity to finally get past the guy in front of us. However, it was a blind, reckless move. It was impossible to see enough of the highway, since we were all traveling up a rise.

The Mustang suddenly spun sideways to the road and then miraculously recovered in the right lane, narrowly averting a head-on collision with 18 wheels of screeching death that had suddenly appeared. The truck jacked dangerously in blue smoke to avoid meeting its end at the hands of a careless Mustang. The truck's driver found his horn too late and blasted it as he straightened his rig and thundered past me.

After watching the young driver in the Mustang use his insolent reflexes to perform this feat, I reacquired my customary state of grace.

With all my might, I shouted:

"Asshole!"

Eventually, I leisurely passed the slower driver on a lengthy stretch of straightaway. When we were alongside each other, I looked at him; it was an odd moment that seemed to hang there indefinitely. A brilliantly strong and vibrant senior face peered at me through the reflecting glass. Perfect teeth behind a striking mustache and a carefully groomed gray beard, shiny baldness aloft. His eyes twinkled as our gazes connected.

It didn't actually occur in his muscles, but something in him winked at me as I passed. He wore a perpetual smile, and though it wasn't for me, it broadened just a tick. Ever so slightly he nodded. I sensed something kindred, as if I'd always known him. Then it was over and I crossed the parade of center-lane stripes. His sleek, modern yellow truck and camper were dwindling in my rearview mirror.

I felt warm.

Staying Awake

Ellen was asleep against the passenger-side window—somehow. This actually surprised me. She hadn't slept in a vehicle for as long as I could remember, not since the day she and the road had collided. So I was left, for a spell, to entertain myself as we zoomed through and away from this dramatic geography we both loved and, surely, always loved in. It was my job to stay awake and alert, to keep us safe from high-speed harms disguised as doldrums and boredom. So I munched on sunflower seeds.

I wasn't returning from the remote regions of the Canyonlands today because I wanted to. Rather, I felt I had to. After all, the world expected a well-paid engineer, successful business owner, and entrepreneur to be at the office. I often made these spontaneous escapes from the city to travel the road but, so far, always returned. Though you wouldn't catch me admitting it, this act of driving home before I was ready nagged that my rebellion might be more on paper than in practice. What would it take to pursue my impulses full force? I wasn't sure I was prepared to find out, lest I end up in free fall; free fall, as in off a cliff.

I'm ripening, I told myself, and time moved swiftly on while I figured out, bit by bit, how to abandon the security of the things I didn't want to do. Anyway, there must be easier transitions from the life I'd settled for to the one I wanted. Cliffs are a nasty business. An easy transition? Why not? Could happen! I didn't think I'd be able to bear any more hard ones where my mirror shatters and those around me are left bleeding from the shards.

However, I did give myself a few good marks for progress. Wasn't I more independent than the average wage earner I was driving home to rub shoulders with? Hadn't I skipped out in this non-holiday zone to take a brilliantly unplanned and unexpected trip? Never mind the penalties piling up, which I would obediently pay upon returning. This trip was symbolic, my assertion that there was more than enough time, an abundance of dollars, and that I had the freedom to do what I wanted. But the assertion was lame; I wasn't liberated, not nearly. I had taken only a week. I'd wanted to take the rest of my life.

Problem was, that wasn't the whole story. At least not this time. Spontaneity wasn't solely to blame for my being on the road. By now, those at home were probably frantic. To them, I had simply vanished seven days ago.

But in those seven days, something else had vanished.

In a merciful way, the reason that had actually triggered this journey had also gone missing. It was absent from the world of my consciousness, and I wasn't about to disturb the ground where it laid buried, lest I dare it to surface.

It was amazing, in general, how little I comprehended of what was going on. I should have, since the signs were all around me. I had set something in motion, something non-physical, and now things were happening so sideways that they made no sense at all to my fiercely linear mind. So this new ability to utterly erase black events from my mind, considering all that had transpired of late, would be a shocker that was just going to have to get in line behind all the others.

It had been like finally arriving at that extravagant restaurant, the one you had always heard of, always dreamed of affording, where any desire is served, placing an order for crème brulee and getting chopped liver.

That's not what I asked for. And this stuff would gag a vulture.

So, I tried applying a little faith. Perhaps chopped liver somehow led to crème brulee. Perhaps I needed chopped liver on the path to crème brulee. I did get something when I placed an order, right? Didn't that at least prove the restaurant was serving?

Okay then, I'll keep at it.

Or am I kidding myself? I really would rather have crème brulee.

Naw, go on, keep at it.

The alternative was despair. I've tried despair, and that's a dark meat grinder of ever denser chopped liver from which no light escapes.

I preferred to believe I could get what I wanted. I just hadn't deciphered the menu yet.

But at this table I was being served some weird stuff, and worse yet, I had the distinct feeling I was being fed it by the teaspoon. Later, it would be by the bucketful, then— *tremor*— something avalanche this way comes.

For the present, I was quite content getting smaller portions, thank you very much, especially when it took only a teaspoon's worth to deliver an ancient boulder unto my mortal flesh.

So I pondered the climbing mishap again. At the same time, I dropped my wounded arm from the steering wheel to my lap, since it was hurting. Though my stiff abdomen awaited final diagnosis, I believed it was in the clear; no blood had shown up in my stools. I was surprised I hadn't scared Ellen to death. Why did that accident happen? And why didn't it go more badly, as it had every right to?

The day before yesterday, in that near-vertical chute of red stone, I had readied myself for the extreme time span, depravation, and hardship of a wilderness rescue.

It's a certainty that Ellen will have to leave me here, I was already thinking, seconds after the rock that hit me disappeared beneath us. We heard it crashing down unseen cliffs. It would be two hours, at least, for her to get back to our off-road camp and collect our vehicle, and then six to eight hours of extremely technical four-wheel driving on a route laden with treacherous, slick rock bluffs and roadless passes. Since it was already afternoon, that would have to be negotiated in the dark. No, it would be tomorrow morning at least before rescuers arrived, and if I was bleeding internally?

Carrying an injured man out on a trail is arduous, taking several strong bodies and substitutes enough to switch off—getting one out of a semi-technical climb like this was, well, unimaginable. I tenderly tested my hurt arm after the initial salvo of pain had passed, feeling for breaks. I couldn't tell a thing, except it screamed not to be touched. However, it was my abdomen, and the organs therein, that concerned me most.

I looked up at the thin line of blue sky formed a hundred feet above, between the two red walls, and lay there. We were on a small ledge in a cliff formation that climbers call a chimney. My back was against one cool wall, and my torso was angled to keep my legs straight and my ruined belly as flat as possible in the narrow confine. Ellen was unnaturally calm as she hovered over me. We exchanged no words. I uttered a few grunts that indicated my injuries, and she seemed to understand. She was occupied, active around me. But doing what, I didn't know. Could I have survived this without her?

After what seemed an eternity but was probably less than an hour, I started rejecting the idea of rescue from this remote aerie. I attempted to stand. At first my abs buckled in protest. Eventually, though, they supported the upright position. The arm could take no weight, however.

We had gone only a short distance up this chimney, so

looking down, there was just a 12-foot vertical descent. I was trying to think how to grab handholds below me without two hands.

I faced into the chimney's dark crevice and experimented using the shoulder of my damaged arm on one wall while counterforcing against the other wall with my feet. In that manner I could span the two walls and hold myself at an angle.

I thought this position might work to inch my way down, but it made me blind to the knobs and ledges I'd need for steps. Ellen passed me to the inside, making her way to the chimney floor. From there she started talking me through the climbing moves. Facing into the crevice, as I was, I couldn't see her. Perhaps it was the way the chamber reflected sound, in an eerie way, that made it feel as if her words were inside my head rather than coming from below me.

Less than an hour ago I would have blasted down this section in three quick motions, without a single thought. Now I was reduced to the pace of a snail, each painful movement demanding absurd concentration. I reached with my right foot, blindly tested the rock wall below. It felt smooth and endlessly vertical.

"There's a knob just six inches below," Ellen's voice whispered.

I stretched farther, straining with my toes. Nothing stopped my foot. Suddenly, I was slipping. My right shoulder lost contact with the wall, and my shirt came apart as the sandstone tore at it. There was no returning to that securely wedged position I was sliding away from. The chute below me opened wider. I fell backward.

"Three points of contact at all times. Never make a dynamic move when you climb." It was the first rule of safe rock climbing, learned from day one. Too late! I had committed myself. My body was going down. I felt the alarming surge of weightlessness.

Abruptly, my left foot contacted the small protruding knob on the otherwise-sheer wall, the one that my right foot had missed. This stopped my fall but not my stomach. If there was such a thing as luck, that was luck.

The shoulder of my damaged arm immediately re-engaged the opposite wall. Rock scraped deeply into skin that was now exposed by my newly ripped shirt. I felt moisture there but didn't look to see if that was from sweat or blood.

It occurred to me then that I might be making my situation considerably worse and I wondered if descending was the correct decision after all.

Ellen said I was nearly down and told me to stretch my next foot backward. There was a ledge directly behind and below. This was going to be another reach of faith, since I couldn't see what I was to place my foot on. But I didn't hesitate.

I made my leg long, longer. There was nothing there. I had no more length. I also had no other choice. With Ellen's encouragement, I un-wedged my shoulder from its new perch and this time deliberately fell backward with foot extended rearward. In less than two inches my foot pounded safely on something solid. With one more step I was below the 12-foot section of wall that marked the location of my climbing disaster.

I collapsed to the ground and waited until my outraged broken places stopped screaming so loudly.

The next challenge was a tunnel maze formed by car-size boulders piled in a crevice. We had ascended this earlier. It consisted of 60 vertical feet of turns, twists, and squeezing between layers of shelf and sandstone ceilings. I recalled it had begun with an 18-foot technical wall that included a small leap and grab. I feared that wall more than anything else. It would be impossible to descend there and reverse the required movement with just one good arm.

I climbed down and worked my way through the labyrinth of piled boulders. Cool rock that never saw the desert sun kissed my cheeks as I used opposing positions that tore at my wrecked belly. Necessity held my abdominal tissue together through the seemingly endless sequence of required moves, and at the bottom I waited once again while the pain ebbed.

We had arrived at the top of the 18-foot impasse.

"I'm not getting down that, Ellen." I felt defeated.

"I know," she answered. Ellen wiped the sweat from my brow with her cotton sleeve, then petted me. I laid my head in her lap and let her comfort me.

"You'll get out of this, babe." Her voice was soothing, like an angel. "I know how much it hurts, and that's not going to change any time soon. But you're incredibly strong."

I put my good arm around the shaded cool skin of her thigh, below her shorts.

"I can't believe this is happening," I told her.

"Trust, honey." Her voice was like the gentle cooing of a mourning dove. "Good will come from this, even if it doesn't make sense now."

Okay, that's absolutely ridiculous. You're going too far, I thought, but didn't speak it. No good can possibly come from this. This is a horrible accident! That's all! Nothing more!

She was looking around. She seemed to be calculating.

Fine—I couldn't move anyway. I was going to need some time here.

"I'll be back," she said all of a sudden. Then Ellen left me without another word, disappearing through a light shining from the center of the dark labyrinth above and behind us.

She was gone for an eternity. The sun was moving into the last quadrant of the sky and was beginning to vanquish my cool shade. Even this early in the spring, the desert sun had tremendous punch. The rock wall behind me began to reflect and then amplify the heat.

From where I lay, I could see down to one of the straw-colored grassland parks far below. It was opposite of where our camp would be.

The park was remarkably flat-bottomed land, narrow and quite long, between two 50-foot-high, sheer-cliff sandstone ridges. It had a definite trail of red sand running through its center. At the other end of the park sprang a ghoulish ridge of needles and spires, unbelievably tall, as if transported from some crimson Martian landscape.

As I watched, a white-tailed deer, then her doe, moved like tiny specks onto the trail.

By the time the deer abandoned the park, I was recovered sufficiently, and loneliness descended upon me. I couldn't stand to be without Ellen. I was broken, and she held me together. Where was she? What if she wouldn't be able to come back anymore? What if it was finally over? I couldn't accept that. I needed her badly and felt an unnatural panic mounting.

When I thought I couldn't stand the separation a second longer, she was there again, as if appearing out of thin air.

"I have another way down." She was smiling at me, and I fell into her eyes.

I came to appreciate the fortuity it must have taken to discover the alternate path down, offering a way to avoid the 18-foot cliff. She guided me back to a hidden route that was at the midpoint of the 60-foot labyrinth. I hadn't noticed it before because its entry just looked like a dead end. Its existence amazed me. I was in no shape to fully understand it. I could never have found the passage by myself, especially in my broken state.

Once we were out of the labyrinth, the path gradually slanted to occasionally walkable, where it had been only climbable above. Ellen came across a most improbable patch of snow hiding in a deep shadow. This snow would be gone in 48 more hours of the springtime desert heat. It shouldn't have been there in the first place. What a gift, what a confirmation, but of what?

I had a plastic bag in my day pack, and we scooped as much snow as would fit in it. A few more 45-degree slots, with easier scrambling, and we were down into the huge whale's-mouth formation that shaded our large tent. In the cool sand were also several fold-up chairs, scattered gear, and, finally, our trusted titan, the powerful, dark-blue Land Cruiser.

I grabbed one of the chairs waiting under the cavernous shade created by the mammoth rock overhang and dragged it with my good arm into the sun. As I plopped down and sank into the supple canvas, it slowly dawned on me: I had escaped doom.

However, I wasn't at all well, and my injuries worried me. So I traded the pain of crushed organs and ligaments for the torture of ice, freezing the cells around my injured parts. I sat shivering and basking as the last hours of sun worked to warm me. Ellen was beside me, sitting shadowed on an adjacent rock. She had removed her shoes and socks and was toeing the sand in respectful but impenetrable silence.

"So what's the point? What are we getting at?" I begged the cloudless, searing blue sky for an answer. While sitting there, I wondered if I would have to be driven to a hospital. That would be of much lesser consequence than the wilderness rescue I had originally organized in my mind. Yet I knew that even an emergency-room visit wouldn't be necessary. The way my body was starting to respond, I might even be hitting the trails by tomorrow, albeit stiffly.

"So what's the point?"

What I couldn't shake was the growing feeling that I had somehow chosen this mishap. I hadn't realized it before, but now, back at camp, it seemed I had caused it, almost deliberately. As I sat there recovering, I went over that critical moment of the climb in my mind, over and over.

"Whoa, this baby's loose!" Ellen called down as she had ascended the chute ahead of me. It was a huge chock stone above her, pressed between the left and right vertical walls.

"For Chrissakes, chimney over it. Don't touch it," which she easily did.

We don't take risks, haven't for years. We're not newbies. There are a lot of wilderness miles in our combined resumes. Yet when I climbed up to the same point, something primordial inside me took over and did the most horrifying thing. Looking back, I couldn't believe it—I don't think that was really me. It was like watching someone else as my own hand reached and tested the little wedge stone that kept the boulder above me in place. My mind rushed in to stop that insane hand from tinkering with the supporting wedge.

Too late. The boulder had begun to move.

I adjusted the dripping snow-ice bag to keep it engaged simultaneously on my broken gut and my swollen arm.

"Why? What's the point?" I asked the infinite. "I don't get it. Had I been asleep?"

Nothing.

"Well, you have my attention now!"

From the searing blue sky came only silence.

Travel Games

I rocketed down the roadway, man's greatest expression of freedom, back toward civilization, man's cauldron for creation. My mind was clear and vibrant after a week in the canyons. I was reluctant to return where I would resume occupations that, although loaded with merit, left me tired and spinning in the evenings. In this clean Canyonland desert, my energy had been inexhaustible.

Ellen shifted on her pillow against the window as I expertly cracked a sunflower seed, retrieved its meat, and ejected the shell in one motion. For a moment I was concerned the sound might have awakened her. But she stopped stirring, for which I was glad. I was actually enjoying the solitude. Not wanting to tempt fate, I left the bag of seeds alone.

It was time to play Shut-the-Frick-Up. This was the fabulous new road game I'd invented, fun for highways, freeways, and even short commutes, where I tried not to think thoughts. I don't know about other people, but I'm so mind-dominant—or is it headstrong?—that the universe can't get a word in edgewise. So I devised this pastime where I try to travel the distance between two mile-marker posts without thinking something, about 53 seconds at my present speed. I had been practicing for several months but had yet to make it even a quarter of the distance.

To be honest, with all those thoughts whizzing around like a convention of 2-year-olds, every moment of every day, my head needed a rest. But more than that, I wanted to hear something other than my mind's prattle, and I entertained myself for hours on the road as I attempted it.

Let's see, okay, Mile Marker 24 — **GO!** —

> *Vehicle bounces. Body swaying. Scenery reels*
> *in gentle hues. Seductive white stripes from*
> *the road flicker.*
> *Shrill screech erupts under the hood.*

I'll have to replace that air-conditioner compressor.

Won't be cheap. Won't be a problem if Unity Semiconductor places their order. In fact, think of the bucks I could put away if they *do* place the order. If they don't, how am I even going to make it to December?

THINKING!

I caught my mind starting to chatter. So I put a label on the thought process.

WORRY

Labeling my thoughts usually puts an end to them. All that remains, to get back in the game, is to clear my mind with a zap.

ZAP.

Picket line of guardrail posts strobing light.
Yellow clumps of buffalo grass bend in gentle
breeze. In the distance, a wooden road sign,
small blotch that grows.
Sign for the Mormon Trail.

That way you can get up to Arch Canyon.

Golden grass between red ruts that meander
north ...

We went there that one April when it was hotter than hell.

... as horizon pans, distance cliffs red against
sapphire mountains.

Then we bugged out and headed to the cooler high country, through the Bears Ears, into the aspen. David was 2, in his child car seat, and we drove around at night on critter hunts counting 30 or 40 deer, and some ringtails, too. I would flash the deer with my handheld floodlight while I drove, and their eyes would reflect like small lanterns, bewitching the forest. The three of us would squeal in delight, and David Jr. with his tiny finger would point. "Deer eyes," he would say. ...

THINKING!
DWELLING IN THE PAST
ZAP.

Mile Marker 25
... Frick, restart.

Engine purrs. Head jerks as front tire flies
over pothole.

He is really screwing me, and his ability to rationalize it,
so he can live with himself, I suppose, is stunning.

THINKING!
FEAR OF OTHERS
ZAP.

Mile Marker 26
... Frick, restart.

Reflected sunlight dances across seats as air
conditioner caresses. Juniper trees waltz be-
fore scarlet cliffs to the hum of the road.

This feels great.

I want to feel this more often. I'd like to have so much
time that everything is a pleasure. A typical Monday morning
ought to start with placing a new belt on the sander, turning
the machine on, and coming inside to have a cup of coffee
with Ellen while the belt crowns. Then have a leisurely morning
learning how to use that Shop Smith, patiently crafting and
molding hardwoods—

Maybe spend the afternoon in the recording studio.

THINKING!
IMAGINING
Approved use of mind power, but not now.
ZAP. *ZAP.*

How much would it take to do this all the time? I can't possibly wait until I'm 65. It has to be now. How much would I need in the bank, $1 million, $2 million? With today's economy, $2 million, I believe. I'd really have to rev the business up to get it to sell for that.

THINKING!
FEAR OF MONEY and WORRY
ZAP.

Mile Marker 27
... Frick, restart.

> *Wheels rumble, muted rumble.*
> *Rumble ... rumble.*

Wow, I've gone a long time without thinking.

THINKING!
THINKING ABOUT THINKING
ZAP.

Mile Marker 28

> *In my lane ahead, a white sedan. White bumper, white car, blue bumper sticker squarely in the back window.*

I don't put bumper stickers on my vehicle. Unfair or not, the car's owner can become lesser having placed a bumper sticker for the eyes of the road. "Here's everything I am! Reduce me to this single statement; squeeze me into six or seven words!"

I've seen some owners attempt to avoid a stereotype by plastering several stickers on their cars. But alas, the ideas are usually a consistent theme that all too often invites silent contempt from driving multitudes who disagree. In a sense, the owner of the bumper sticker fired the first shot. Pasting up the sign was a hostile act. Not to mention that it presents a road hazard, with tailgaters trying to read the small text.

The exception, I suppose, might be humor—such as "Imagine Whirled Peas." But even as I chuckle at that, I realize it's derogatory. I've yet to see a solitary idea that I would place on my bumper to represent me.

I pushed on the accelerator and approached the white sedan long enough to read the offering.

CHRIST SUFFERED FOR YOU.

For heaven's sakes! I backed off the white sedan.

If the Christ himself were tooling around the desert on this sunny afternoon in a white sedan, is that the vital message he would beam to the world, "I suffered for you"? Somehow, I doubted it.

Memories from an altar boy slipped into my head. I was wearing a cassock robe under a white linen surplice, swinging smoking incense from a chain in my hand, piously following the priest, a small group of faithful following us around the inner perimeter of the cathedral for Stations of the Cross. As had been practiced for a millennium, we paused at each heart-wrenching scene of the Christ's suffering. My young heart dutifully attempted to empathize at each image—to try to feel what it would be for me to be betrayed, scourged, beaten, nailed, daggered, and murdered.

But before even finishing high school, I bounced fairly hard off that particular emphasis from my Catholic upbringing. Perhaps it was just my take, but it seemed as if the significance of Christ had been diminished in Christendom's struggle to reconcile his end. I couldn't believe that the Christ intended us to focus on that. Did his Father need him to suffer for our sins? We do that for ourselves—all too well.

Someone, somewhere, show me a better précis that the Christ would stick on his bumper, or the Buddha, Muhammad, the Dalai Lama—distill it into one eye-popping, universally endearing phrase, and that sign I will glue to my car.

Hmmm ... how about a bumper sticker with three simple words for every onlooker: "I love you."

Yeah, right—you'd have to be Jesus Christ or something.

> *Chunk-chunk from the road, as tires fly over*
> *a cattle guard.*

I shook my head. "Well, out of the game by now, aren't we, David?" I whispered to myself. That was quite a tour de force of thinking. Damn, I'd really like to shut my thinker down, just for once.

Now was as good a time as any. I took a deep breath to try again.

Mile Marker 42

... Restart.

> *My lungs inhale. Mountains, sky exhale. Only*
> *my breath, only Canyon's breath, only breath.*

Mile Marker 43

Mile Marker 44

Mile Marker 45

Mile Marker 46

Mile Marker 47

—The Christ knew no pain, only joy.

What?

I brushed the game aside.

How could that be possible?

If the Christ performed miracles—no delay between intending something and its appearance—that would indicate an immovable connection to source, the highest of vibrations. The one able to raise Lazarus wouldn't be burdened by life, as are we.

But no pain? What of the Passion?

My brain seized possession of the paradox that had parachuted into my head, unconcerned about from where it might have come.

What *do* I know?

Well, I know that I've made myself miserable by the way I've thought about things, or when I was out of harmony with the natural flow. Couldn't imagine the Christ bothering with any of that! I know that by believing in the sorrows surrounding us, we join them. But I've always held that those of special grace attain the unattainable because earthly conditions have no power over them.

Suddenly, I couldn't reconcile how the Christ could walk on water and, in the same light, experience doubt or succumb to despair. What have we done to him?

What am I missing?

—There is no pain ... only joy.

Huh? Am I to believe that?

That's not my experience. Flesh knows pain. I know suffering, real suffering. Even if it's because I allow it, believe me, there's pain—guaranteed. I know I inflict it on others, too. And bear witness to the shattering of my world. Was that a choice? No! Pain couldn't be more real.

—Then there is no joy ... only pain.

Look, you can't have it both ways. It has to be one or the other.

—Exactly.

That stopped me. For a while, I heard only the sounds of my vehicle on the road, felt the sun through the window, the terrain of the path as conveyed in the gentle rocking, lifting, and falling of my seat.

Eventually I pondered it one step further. Don't we have both joy and pain?

—Can you be at both ends of a rod?

I hurt.

—Can a light be on and off?

But I hurt so deeply. Help me excuse it.

—There is only light, or its absence.

Who has turned off my light?

—Who else could?

No—

Mile Marker 125

THINKING!

—*has blocked the voice communicating to you.*

Communicating to... Holy cow! Was that from outside of me?

Wait!

Come back.

I'm listening...

Mile Marker 126

... Frick, restart.

Highway Conditions, Road Closures

Amazing how fast the landscape could speed past in this era of man. Today, in driving mode—as opposed to the hiking mode I'd been in the previous five days—I released the details of cedar mesa, missed the small creatures and intricate canyons in a blur of motion, but gained some vision of a larger scheme. Out my window lay a garden of stone, immense in proportion. Red fins jutted from cliff walls, some becoming as narrow as a man's outstretched arms, all of them towering to the sky, forming a jagged frame around a masterpiece of freestanding monoliths and hoodoos that in turn dwarfed the road streaming through them. These monuments of stone were enthroned on high escarpments; each alone was wonderment. Hordes of them zooming past at 60 miles an hour were downright supernatural. On foot, this area would be a maze to traverse for days. On spinning wheels it held just a bit part in a larger performance. For this colossal maze of monuments, in front of their tall red cliffs, was but the downstage of my Canyonland theater.

Above the cliffs rose an upper basin whose lips curled with swirling white-cedar mesa sandstone, forming colorless breasts and gentle rolling mounds known as slick rock. The ravines and perimeter of the slick rock were decorated with twisted juniper and sturdy piñon, picking a living out of the heat. Green lines formed by these desert-dwelling trees drew the eye away toward blue mountains that sprang from red desert. Up there, cool tall pine and pale aspen lived with no thought of their scorched brothers below.

All these individual features of this vast terrain were compressed by my road and by my velocity, which distorted time so that I could take in all the land at once, as would a god.

Previous inhabitants of this country, whose trails and remains I always found in the remote canyons, would never comprehend this road of mine. In my mind, as I drove, I fancied I could yank those prior incarnations of man out of time and place them behind this or that escarpment up ahead.

Imagine the simple ancient, a basket-maker perhaps, harvesting yucca fiber for a new pair of sandals, maybe a defensive cliff dweller ever timid and afraid of his world anyway, or later a member of the People, nomads from the north, hunting in the piñon and juniper. Perhaps even a bold and righteous Mormon pioneer might peer out from behind the rock.

All would be awestruck to see my machine flying by on a 20-foot-wide extension of mankind's claim into the natural wilderness. Were those people from those other ages that much different from me? Or were they the same humans at a different speed? Though most of them had only half my life span, did they live longer because life was slower?

I've also often wondered what it would be like if I could peer out from behind that rock up ahead and see me driving by when I was younger, or when I'm older. Meet myself on the road, as it were.

For some reason that I never got around to questioning, I often thought of this. Sometimes I'd even catch myself idly looking around at a familiar corner, street, or road, almost expecting to catch a glimpse of a previous me, with no real resistance to the idea.

It made Einsteinian sense, I suppose. His discoveries in relativity showed travel into the future or the past to be quite possible, just not in any way feasible—at least not without draining two months of the Earth's total power output—and not yet practical for anyone wishing to take his mortal body along.

Einstein once said that no matter how persistent the illusion may be, *the distinction between past, present and future is nonetheless, only illusion*. I liked that, since our customary notion of time, at the moment, was a prison for me.

Was it possible to jump around in time without traveling at the speed of light or being squished in a black hole? I didn't know. But time travel into the future is actually commonplace. We humans have been moving steadily into our future since creation. However, moving appreciably faster than others into the future might prove more difficult. That is, of course, unless time didn't actually exist. This would be a good trick to play on us.

I also noted that I knew how to go back in time without any difficulty. I did it often. It was called remembering. And at this moment it was quite simple to travel back, since I had been on this stretch of highway so many times in my past.

If I blurred my eyes and concentrated, I could easily pass my earlier self, a previous vehicle, a different job, a wholly different set of troubles, but the same yearnings. With this feat of memory I could see how I, *how we*, since Ellen was always there, looked back then, sense how we felt.

There we were in a K5 Blazer, cracked frame and bailing wire, that certainly shouldn't be as far from a mechanic as it was. My hair was longer. I believe we were having one of those earth-scorching arguments. Nope, she was reading to me, lovingly, while I drove. I would've liked to offer some advice to that younger us, now that I knew how impotent the things that scared or angered us turned out to be, and how singular and precious every moment actually was.

Or maybe I could look out to see my next older self driving past.

"What will life be like a year from now?" my business partner was fond of asking, whenever we were struggling with some unyielding burden that made our days endless and difficult.

Ellen would say that if I keep thinking the way I do, I'll end up an insufferable, nostalgic old geezer. Why not? I've always been a nostalgic young geezer.

I experienced a minuscule sensation of weightlessness as our vehicle dropped into the dip of a desert wash.

WATCH FOR FLASH FLOODS, a sign in the arroyo read.

That was a pretty ridiculous warning, in my experience. Not that I hadn't been in a flash flood before. It's just that there was nothing to watch out for; you're just all of a sudden in it. They can come from nowhere in the canyon desert, and sometimes the horizon doesn't require a rain cloud in sight to produce them. That terrifying and beautiful natural event is rare. Rarer are those who have actually experienced them.

However, I had discovered a few steps one could follow to ensure you're squarely bulldozed by one. For starters, you could make a permanent camp in the bottom of a dry desert gorge without giving a thought to what forces carve dry desert gorges.

So, what were the other steps I'd taken to place me in the torrent currently sweeping my life away? Had there been other signs along the way?

How about this early one,

TRAFFIC JAMS ON ALL MAJOR ROUTES

Out of college, as a decently paid working and family man, I would wake up in the morning in time to join the fight on crowded freeways to work, struggle all day to impress co-workers and bosses who were struggling to impress co-workers and bosses. I'd then fight the crowded freeways back home. Back home, I would spend a tired evening squeezing in a bit of living with my wife and kids before hitting the sack to wake up in the morning and notice my life wasn't the one I had in mind.

DETOUR

So I went down to half-time for a spell and tried to make a living from music, which always moved me and for which I had a gift. After all, in college it had been a coin toss between engineering and rock-starring. I had never given up on the music and believed it held some key. So after several years of engineering, I made a serious run at songwriting. Loved the music, hated the business, and though I opened several doors, nobody was buying.

LANES MERGE AHEAD

So I eventually tried doing something different, something bold. After having endured years of half-income during my music foray, I dared to murder all remaining security for my young family and became an entrepreneur, independent, complete with denied terror.

ROAD CONSTRUCTION

It was an absorbing process, for one doesn't take on such perilous risk lightly. I would wake up earlier and go in later to avoid the time everyone else traveled to work. But I would also come home much later, with even less time to squeeze in some tired living with my wife and family. So demanding was this endeavor that it took a long time to notice that I was waking up in the morning to the same old life and not the one I had in mind.

But, of course, I was now free of others' scripts, no longer punching the clock, in an incredibly creative, potentially lucrative, if not demanding, life. So this would surely lead to what I sought,

> eventually,
> ultimately,
> sooner or later,
> in due course,
> as time goes by ...
> ticktock

SLIPPERY WHEN WET

So I plunged my head into the stream even harder. Consequently, it was a long time indeed until I noticed I was waking up each morning to the same old life and not the one I had in mind.

I wasn't, by any means, the only malcontent wandering the career corridors. There were more than a few of us wanna-be-elsewheres. We were all seemingly resigned to earning our daily bread and paying for our cars in the traditional manner. All the while, we were intangibly shamed by the hordes who were actually content to be there at work.

One such fellow malcontent was Tommy Eckle, the slump-shouldered, good-natured, though rather mediocre engineer who hid behind thick glasses and spoke of wanting nothing more than to compose walls of music for cathedral pipe organs. But on the rare occasions he spoke of it, he would always end by shrugging with no shoulders and smiling sheepishly, as if to apologize for such lunacy.

Across boundaries of earth and time, I'm sure I shared a shadowed meal with a vast table of unknown malcontents. Though there are many who are quite well known. For example, the dissatisfied clergy student-turned-medical student-turned dissenter who enraged his wealthy parentage as he hitched a ride on the HMS Beagle to collect finches. In my faction, it's well understood that those odd successful examples are, to some degree, culpable for the persistence of the rest of us shadowed dreamers.

Aside from Ellen, and excluding my occasional but noticeable forays, I kept all this to myself. My unrest wasn't from being trapped in some occupation; in fact, I had a rather good one. Nor was it from anything else I was doing, for in truth I was having a good life and even a good bit of fun as an entrepreneur.

It was something I wasn't doing that wouldn't let me be. There was something else, though I couldn't be certain just what, or just why. Previous attempts at sedition, such as songwriting, had been like chasing fireflies that winked out as I came near and then reappeared elsewhere as I trampled in pursuit.

All this held for me, as it probably did for my pipe-organing associate, inspiration from the infinite lover. It was a glimpse of how it would feel, but not necessarily what I should do. So now as my clock counted off too many years, I came about to pursue it again, more aggressively, more openly, with finality.

ROAD NOT SUITABLE FOR ALL VEHICLES

So a reasonable question, I suppose, is from where did all this arise? I had encountered an atypical mix of people in my life. Was it they who begat the yearnings, or had the yearnings attracted the unusual company? Probably the latter, since they all seemed familiar as they showed up.

And the first to appear, so long ago, was Futzu. Apart from my days at college, and then again in that brief but startling encounter three years ago, Futzu wasn't really present for that much of my life, though in retrospect it has felt otherwise.

Futzu

"Dying is to life what waking is to sleep," he said, and paused.

Then he added, "I know when I'm going to die."

Was it the way his eyes twinkled, how he acted like someone discussing a shiny new car, that disturbed me as Futzu spoke those words?

No, that wasn't it. By now I was used to his demeanor.

"Life and death are only as different as an inhale and an exhale. We are infinite beings having a finite experience. You can learn this now, while you dream, or at the end when you wake. But either way," he said, chuckling, "you're bound to discover it."

Then his eyes became intense, perhaps urging. "How different would your dream be, though, to know it now?"

What disturbed me was, despite the fact that there were eight of his advanced students sitting in the dusk around him, he was looking at me. At the time, I didn't get it, or tried to ignore the odd sensation that I was being singled out. But I got the strongest notion that his words were specifically addressed to me. But Futzu normally chose his words to establish a lesson, not a message.

I'd remember these words quite differently, though, years later, when their connection to me unfolded.

Everyone waited for Futzu to go on, add something. But he said no more. Perhaps his serenity surrounding the topic had conveyed all that was needed. Anything else would have been superfluous.

The eight of us were dressed in black cotton garments, loose top and pants, with no buttons and closed by a sash. As was required by this ancient tradition of mental, physical, and spiritual training, our sashes were black and tied at the side. Futzu's sash was orange and tied in front.

Futzu, we were told, meant teacher. It was an obscure title that I had never found in another reference. And one had to imagine the Asian ancestry of this art form because it wasn't apparent from Futzu's distinctly Anglo face. But in the winter room there was a tattered black and white picture of our teacher, as a young man, being thrown over the head of a stout, small and completely bald-headed Chinese. That was the master who fled communism and trained Futzu in the late '50s.

There were no other pictures, no photographs of Futzu's childhood spent in a body cast after his pelvis had been crushed under a tractor or any of his long convalescence. Futzu told stories of how, for years, he'd gotten around by walking on his hands. But except for the one faded black-and-white picture, his life was undocumented, unverifiable. Nonetheless, it was certain that his life was different. Even strangers sensed when Futzu walked into a room, before he said a word.

I didn't have to look at the other seven faces sitting around me in the fading light to see them in my mind. I knew each of them from untold hours spent together. Some were in their early twenties, as were Ellen and I, and tolerated sitting cross-legged on the hard driftwood floor with youthful resilience. Others were older and shifted discreetly on numb buttocks to get occasional blood flow.

At least the humbly constructed porch where we now sat was screened. Therefore, the gnats were cleanly absent. An hour ago we had begun this third session of what Futzu called "advanced training" outside sitting on long ponderosa logs in the gathering area. The gnats were particularly bad. They had given me considerable trouble during the 20-minute meditation.

To be honest, I always had some trouble with meditation anyway, but now I was being chewed on. I could feel the blood-sucking bugs crawling in my ears. They were biting in there, too. Many of the stings on the back of my neck were starting to itch irresistibly. But I didn't scratch. It was ridiculous—must my face be turned into a lunar landscape of welts for this compulsory meditation?

As long as possible, I resisted. In through the nose, out through the mouth. Empty the mind of the thoughts flowing in, like pouring out a tea cup. In through the nose, out through the mouth. In through the nose ... I breathed in one of those stinking gnats.

That was it. I couldn't help it. My eyes popped opened. I used a hand to shoo the cloud of microscopic flying insects and sneezed out a gnat pellet.

I snuck a look at Ellen. Her eyes were closed, and her pretty face was twisted with distraction. Obviously, there was no deep mediation going on there.

Next, I gazed across at Dan. From the neck up, he looked the part of a rugged fur trapper, with thick, dusty beard and sunbaked face. But he was dressed like the rest of us, so the analogy ended there. Dan was withstanding the onslaught considerably better, but I did note that a meditative hand rose with meditative slowness to dispatch a few gnats now and again. The others, who sat with me on the circle of logs, were also performing one variation or another of discreet, closed-eye ear rubbing.

Then I looked at Futzu. Gnats covered his peaceful face as well.

Humph, I thought. He has it no better; he's no superhuman. Suddenly, as I watched, all the gnats leaped from his face. It was as if they had been projected by a two-inch force field. They hovered, buzzing at that distance.

That ended that. Any chance of meditating was completely blown. I shut my eyelids and pondered. Must've been a coincidence. Perhaps I imagined it. Sneaking another look, there were no gnats around Futzu at all. His eyes were closed, and he was smiling.

Advanced training was held in the late evening, extracurricular, and by invitation only. This was new. Futzu had never offered such an opportunity before. So Ellen and I accepted, even though we were already traveling from campus into the mountains three times a week for this art form.

On top of college studies, this affair was a lot to take on. And what struggling university kid could afford the gas or the modest tuition? But from the moment of our first interview and acceptance into his small entourage, Futzu inspired commitment. And from this mysterious and demanding tutor, I was learning of, and tapping into, something larger, something he awoke as I practiced his gentle art of parting the clouds. So Ellen and I carpooled with other students from town to make ends meet.

Tonight's advanced training was going a different direction from the first two. Instead of sharing, Futzu was listening to us in the way he did—fully. All the while, he waited patiently for us to listen to ourselves.

John H., the doubter, was talking. I was surprised he had been invited to these sessions. Perhaps Futzu was unaware how disenchanted John was becoming. Even though he had been at it for years and was originally one of the most dedicated, John had started grumbling among us that some of what Futzu taught was suspect.

You didn't have to know John very long before you realized the standards he held himself and everyone else to. He had little use for those who failed his test of values. Perhaps he had originally placed Futzu too high on a pedestal. The more we entered the mystic aspect of this art, the worse John was becoming.

One of John's recent complaints was Futzu's reference to the pearls. Futzu had told us that when he first met the displaced master in the '50s, this art form had never been taught to a westerner. Futzu explained with the philosophy "Sharing knowledge with a westerner is like *throwing pearls to the swine.*"

John later discovered that that reference was from Matthew's Gospel rather than a philosophy of Chinese descent. This and a growing collection of other examples suggested to John that Futzu might have cobbled together his teachings from many sources, rather than its coming from a pure lineage of masters. For him, this diminished its power.

Worse, the spiritual realm of this teaching was not very demonstrable. Had anyone ever seen Futzu in a four-hour meditation, bare-legged on ice and snow, and watched the snow melt around him? Does anyone at all doubt Futzu's story of accepting heroin as part of a lab experiment conducted in the mid-'60s in which Futzu proved that in a spiritual state one will not experience the drug? Futzu says he sees our auras. Who here has honestly ever seen an aura?

John played the lawyer, trying to let his case establish itself, whispering doubt privately into the ears of others, never coming directly out to challenge. It was a slow poison that John offered to anyone who would have it. But tonight, it would come to a point.

"I don't feel what everyone else *claims* to feel in the energy circle," John said.

Futzu had just finished demonstrating the flowing of his chi, first sending his life energy to the left around our circle of joined hands, then to the right. He asked what we had felt.

Had I felt something? I thought so. But it was subtle, more like an expectation tingling through my solar plexus, nothing that could be confirmed or measured. Had one hand felt warmer and the other colder, as others reported? It could be argued that I created any feeling in my head, desired to feel something and therefore did. John spoke for the skeptical western hemisphere of our brains.

"At any rate, there's nothing really happening here with me," John finished.

"Is that so?" Futzu said. The silence that followed was thick and uncomfortable. John sat straight and pious in our customary modified-lotus position, cross-legged with index fingers and thumbs forming the upside-down teardrop in his lap.

And then Futzu did the strangest thing. He baited John.

"I don't believe you're being honest," he said.

John darkened. Above all else, John was proud of his virtue. Futzu knew this. John at first appeared unflappable. He launched a subtle counterattack, "I have many faults, but at least I'm impeccable with my word."

"You are a man of your word?" Futzu asked.

"Yes."

"In that I agree. Strip all else away and what emanates from us is our word. What does this mean, John—to be impeccable with your word?"

"It means I'm honest. You can count on what I tell you." John jabbed at where he thought Futzu was vulnerable.

Futzu's blue eyes bored into John. We waited, holding our breaths. As far as we were concerned, John might as well have just tied his sash knot in the front for a direct and formal challenge.

"No, John, ... *impeccable* means '*without sin*'. Are your words without sin, John?"

John puckered his face in retreat. Something told me he wasn't going to be part of our car pool for much longer.

It would remain to be seen for whose benefit this exchange had occurred, but at the time, I shrugged it off. John's complaint didn't matter much to me. And as far as the energy circle was concerned, I wasn't that enamored with the mystical anyway.

I was here for more practical reasons. For the first time in my life, I was gaining some sense of personal power. Mine was the traditional youthful and struggling soul. But here, I was discovering that perhaps I wasn't the victim of chance but the architect. I really had no idea to what extent this might be true. Nonetheless, I believed I'd pretty much figured it out. Futzu knew better, but he let me carry on anyway.

It was my turn to talk. "Everyone causes their own misery. If you're fat, change your diet, exercise. No money? Get a skill. What you get comes from your choices." Futzu had gotten me going on my hot topic.

"What if you get a brain tumor? Did you choose that? Is that also your doing?" Futzu asked.

"I don't know, but probably, if you're unhappy." I blasted on. "I listen to unhappy people all the time. They can't even hear how it's their own fault, and they're stuck complaining like a broken record. Why get angry at a flat tire, kick and curse it—just change it. We create unhappiness when we don't flow with life."

Now surely Futzu would agree. Wasn't that a pretty good distillation of what I'd learned here?

"You say you listen?" was Futzu's only comment.

Road of Creation

Sometime after college, Ellen and I stopped making the long commute to the mountain ranch. Oddly enough, it was the obligatory phone calls to Futzu that had decided it. Futzu required his students to call prior to missing a class. We had already pared our commitments to once a week, no longer assisting in teaching other classes or with weekend chores on the ranch. But the mental anguish of too often calling in order to be dismissed was the worst of it, and not having to worry about the damn phone call anymore was the biggest relief.

The phone call I got nearly 20 years later was a big surprise.

It was Nora, Futzu's wife. I sort of remembered her from my last days at the ranch, and I guess I'd heard that Futzu had married her before moving to the North.

Ellen looked up at me after I cradled the phone. How Nora had gotten our unlisted number, after so many years of estrangement, was a mystery. It had been a long time since I'd even thought of him.

"You look strange. Who was that?" Ellen asked.

"Francis is dying, and he's asked to see me." Ellen's jaw dropped.

He was succumbing to horribly slow and painful cancer, refusing treatment. I wondered, sadly, if this could possibly be the end Futzu claimed to have foreseen.

Ellen and I decided to buy a single airline ticket so that I could visit the teacher of our youth. I thought it would be my last service to him. This would prove to be exactly opposite of the truth.

I was finally able to depart 10 days later. A kiss goodbye from the car window at the airport's passenger drop-off ramp and I was alone with my thoughts, readying to wait three hours for a seven-hour flight.

As I navigated through the mob in the concourse, I considered the timing of this event. My life had pretty much hit a brick wall of late, and I was feeling absolutely stuck. Now this. What was this?

Finding a seat at my gate, I plopped into a well-worn cushion that had supported hundreds of other travelers in its mono-purposed and underappreciated existence. There I engaged in my favorite pastime, watching individuals in the crowd. Most were waiting in endless rows of airport chairs, some stood in lines, and the rest were either walking to those chairs or to those lines.

This, I decided, was pretty much life in a nutshell.

A small girl, sitting next to an overweight parent, swinging legs too short to reach the floor. Next to them, a young woman reading fiction so she could be distracted from the fiction she lived. Keyed-up professionals, taking full advantage of the moments before the flight, preparing for endless deadlines. Most senior faces looking beaten down by life, though some smiled nostalgically, living in an ever-changing past. Two rebellious toddlers running from a rule-giving Dad, resisting indoctrination.

They won't escape, I thought, none of us have.

I observed some with righteous expressions, some bored, and a few who knew exactly how pretty or handsome they were. But as I sat, I found myself searching for the rare face where I might find that piercing expression of presence, the glow of contentment, the face of Futzu. Instead, what I found was hordes of souls caught by a dream, like me. We really don't know what's going on here, I thought.

As I sat, I tried to separate what Futzu had taught so long ago from what had come since, but I was having difficulty. My paths blended with fuzzy distinction between steps. I'd achieved much, but a restless cork kept popping to the surface, something vital that remained undone.

It was years after Futzu that I learned to practice magic. Perhaps the roots had been with Futzu all along. Perhaps his teachings led to the same place, but in youthfulness I'd missed it. Nonetheless, I arrived with some additional help.

When I was ready, a surprising species of teachers appeared. They called themselves a group consciousness, and they spoke through an attractive middle-aged woman with a curious style of addressing themselves in the plural. "Good morning. We are extremely pleased that you are here. We know you bring much more than those physical bodies you see in your mirrors."

I was sincerely skeptical about the notion, even scoffing. Was she merely a good actress whose face could transform to something else? Or was she truly able to raise her frequency to the vibration where divinity flows to us, freely? But once I heard what she had to say, it no longer mattered how the message was arriving. Its significance was recognized deep within my spirit, like a prophet before me. I knew it was time to pay attention.

A fresh batch of passengers herded past me. I shifted in my cushioned seat to pull my feet out of the aisle, barely noticing them.

"We really, ... *really* ... want you to get this," the nonphysical entity told us, presumably speaking through the woman's voice. "Your mind's images are literally the blueprints from which your world is built."

"Your every thought forms an unbroken prayer which is always, *all ways* answered." They called this a *law*—the law of attraction.

"Even your physicists, as they peer infinitesimally into matter, cannot find matter. Instead, they discover everything is energy—energy at some vibration, and force. Thought and word is what transforms energy into physical reality. You are the leading edge of what we are, creating all reality with your thoughts and words."

Funny, I'd had a lifelong impression that it was *in doing* that I created stuff. Not so, they said. They asserted that doing is how you receive, not how you create. Doing isn't always required.

As a distant speaker barked out another flight announcement, one of the rebellious toddlers ran smack into my leg.

Instead of cowering away, this miniature human paused, looking tentatively up at me, waiting to see how I would respond.

His face was smeared with the same foodstuff that was in his tiny hand, which was now smeared on my pants. I couldn't help it. I laughed with easy surprise. His big lucid eyes grew even bigger and he squealed with delight. Then he smeared my other leg as he exited my neighborhood of airport seats. I winked good-naturedly at his embarrassed father, waving off his apology. Then I wiped at the jelly-type substance the child had left on my pants, using a napkin that happened to be in the seat adjacent to mine.

That was a match, I thought. I attracted a gooey and charming encounter without doing a thing.

Once I had started paying attention, I discovered that everything in my life had indeed been a match for the rambunctious or conflicted images in my mind. Plus, my life had been busy. I battled upstream.

So, on a cue from this new instructor, I turned downstream. I decided to pay attention to how I thought and spoke to the world, attract differently. Perhaps Futzu would have called it "polishing my mirror."

As my flight was announced, I stood, proudly displaying the streaks of jelly that now marked and separated me from the crowd. I shouldered my small bag and joined the line at my gate.

I was grateful to that spirited teacher. She helped me recognize my true aspirations. It became clear to me what I aspired to be—one who acts magically from source. But to be a sorcerer, one starts as an apprentice. Not an apprentice to her—I didn't know her—so I indentured myself to Source, in whatever form it chose to take.

Magic began to occur, potent magic to be sure.

For instance, I'd always desired to live in the mountains. So I built a wonderful mountain home, ignoring observations that I couldn't at all afford it. Apprentices have help, and in this case it was Ellen. She encouraged me to stop stumbling where money was involved, change my expectations. To my delight, I eventually received a raise to easily cover the mortgage. Sometime after that, as an entrepreneur, I paid off the whole property in one fell swoop. Before, it was unimaginable that I might produce an extra couple of hundred thousand dollars in a year to accomplish such a feat. I discovered that one of my biggest obstacles had been in not believing I deserved it.

I was getting over that.

I retrained my subconscious in other ways, too, since it had been programmed to believe good fortune wasn't sustainable. It was.

I placed an order for a less restrictive work schedule once I decided it was okay. That certainly occurred. I found an immaculate pre-owned diesel truck in just the color, just the features, and nearly the mileage that Ellen and I had written on a sushi-bar paper place mat. The truck traveled 700 miles to be in my driveway, where it sits today, and I still have that soy-sauce-stained place mat in my nightstand drawer.

I had become a successful creator, having unraveled perhaps the biggest mystery of life.

Now, here in the airport, the long quiet voice of Futzu asked from inside me, "And so?"

Their bed-and-breakfast was in an abundant forest well off the beaten path. It was immaculate and picturesque. Tremendous and loving effort had gone into the property. A small stream ran alongside the two-story stone house and slowly spun a large water wheel attached at the side. The sign above the entry read "The Heart Mill."

Nora had aged well. She was younger than Francis, closer to my age than his. She greeted me with a hug of familiarity and asked how Ellen and I were enjoying empty-nesting now that our kids had both moved away. She knew me better than I knew her, which I couldn't fathom, and this made me uncomfortable.

Nora led me into the common area. It was an antique cottage room, log ceiling, stone walls, empty fireplace, and ultramodern wood flooring. It was charming, as was Nora, who asked if I would like some tea. I told her I would prefer to visit Francis.

"You should sit down," Nora said. I reluctantly sank in the deep-pillowed leather couch.

"Francis has been unconscious for more than a day," she told me. "I'm afraid he won't be able to talk to you."

I felt harpooned; I also felt relieved. "Why didn't you call and tell me?"

She shrugged, brushing away a pool of water that had gathered in her eyes. I gave her a moment.

"It's caught me by surprise," she explained. "I've been procrastinating. He had me expecting something different. Now I don't know. He slipped further. Perhaps it's too late."

Before entering his bedroom, Nora had tried to prepare me, but I was still taken aback. I looked down at the slight man lying on his back in the middle of his bed, a shadow of the man I had known. He used to tell his students he didn't have to make his bed in the morning because he didn't toss and turn in his sleep. It wasn't a boast; he was teaching by example, demonstrating the unfettered life, a target for us. "I lie down, close my eyes, and then open them. It's morning. No wrinkles on my bedsheets. I brush the covers and start my day. " He would pantomime the routine while grinning.

There were no wrinkles on his sheets now, immobile on the bed as he was. He lay gaunt and perfectly still. The only sign of life was a slight rasping breath.

What was I doing here? He had known hundreds of others better than me.

Nora gasped from my side, because as we watched, Futzu's eyes popped open, vibrant and clear. He was looking at me.

"There you are."

As those words came from Francis's lips, years of separation dissolved.

Crosses Alongside the Road

I leaned on the steering wheel and waited. Francis had his eyes closed and was experiencing pain. He didn't look like a man suffering, just preoccupied. It was hard to believe his withered body was sitting in the passenger seat of my rental car. He had explained that there was a place he wanted to visit—*one last time.*

When Futzu first awoke on his bed with a "there you are" on his lips, I couldn't think of what to say. "How are you?" probably wouldn't have been a good choice. His condition was all too obvious. I felt awkward and was struck dumb.

For the longest time he lay there taking deep breaths, eyes closed for the inhale, looking at me while he exhaled. Slowly, he worked an elbow up in the direction of his shoulder and pushed himself higher onto his pillow. "I think I'd like to go for a drive now," he said in his hoarse whisper, as if nothing could be more natural. I can't say I was surprised. His demeanor hadn't changed.

I didn't take his words literally. I just thought, sadly, it doesn't appear you'll be going anywhere, Francis; not anymore, not this life.

His blue eyes, alive and piercing as I'd ever known, danced with humor and seemed to warn: don't underestimate me.

Nora walked into the room and brushed past with a glass of cloudy purple juice. I hadn't realized she'd left. She sat on the bed and began nursing liquid into him.

"You're standing there like a dummy," Nora told me. "Sit down."

Futzu cracked a weak smile under the glass, and a bit of juice dribbled down his chin. She set the tumbler down and produced a kerchief to wipe with.

I perched myself awkwardly on the edge of a comfortable-looking chair, next to his bed.

"You scared me, Francis," she said to him. He reached up to her busy hand and she stopped fussing with him.

"Feeling purty good," he said. "Had a nice rest." His chest moved up and down with effort. I felt like an intruder as she bent to embrace him.

"Look who you've brought." Futzu turned to welcome me.

I felt my face go warm with excess blood and finally gave hellos and stood to squeeze the hand of my mentor of old.

"Don't get too comfortable," Futzu croaked as I returned to the chair. "I don't want to visit here in this stuffy ol' room."

I found myself perched uncertainly on the chair's edge once again.

"Is it a good day for a drive?"

I expected some rational protest, or at least a sound "pooh-poohing" from Nora, but none came. She bent toward him and said, "Yes, it's a lovely day."

The room fell silent, waiting.

I hesitated.

Then I slowly rotated my left hand up from my knee to the ceiling and said, "Okay. If you think so. I mean, sure, road trip—my favorite thing."

Nora smiled and swung her legs off the mattress. She asked me to help remove his garments. As I stood, I noticed a stack of clothes folded at the foot of his bed, as if prepared previously—as if I was playing a part in something scripted. All the actors seemed to know their parts and have their lines; all, that is, except me.

Nora sponge-bathed Futzu, and then she and I dressed him. That's when reality gradually returned; it entered through my nostrils from his bed-sore, dank, and diapered body.

At first he had no strength. As I braced his clammy back, I couldn't help feeling this was a terrible mistake, but as we clothed him, some color restored and he actually started helping under his own power, such as it was. This strength must have been pulled from the ether. For it was hard to see how any could derive from his languished body and a few swigs of purple juice.

It required a fireman carry for Nora and me to get Futzu to the car. I could tell that hurt him by the way he stiffened under my arms. His jaw dropped slightly, forming a soundless moan. He endured the transport to the passenger seat of my rental car and then sagged against the headrest.

Nora hung over him fastening a seat belt. A single tear

made a line down her cheek and Francis reached to put a cupped hand over it. They looked into each other's eyes for the longest time.

Then she stood looking at me with a graceful hand on her hip.

"Be back shortly, Nora," I told her.

"I know," she said.

I must have looked at her funny, because she felt the need to add something. "We've already said our goodbyes."

That comment couldn't have been more out of place, but I didn't question it, since more tears were forming on her face. She thanked me. Naturally, I mistook the reason why.

So we went for a drive in the amazing country where Futzu now lived. He watched intently from the passenger window as if he was seeing Alaska for the first time, even though he'd live here for years.

His strength grew as we rode roller-coaster mounds of the frost-heaved road.

"Well, Hoch San," he addressed me with my old student title, "what have you been doing?"

To start, we chitchatted, but I had something I really wanted to share with my old tutor. In due course, the conversation led to the path I was on.

I told him how I was learning to manifest in my life and gave him many examples. I wanted him to be proud of my accomplishments, how things that he'd initiated had progressed for me.

"It's straightforward enough," I explained. "I identify what I want and imagine nothing else, nothing to the contrary. In fact, I act as if it already is. Then it eventually appears, in its own time, through its own doors, but it appears."

I told him I compared this practice to what those on a religious path call prayer; its achievement is from what they call faith. In any event, the world is no more complicated than that. It functions that way because of a physical law of attraction.

Francis listened to me carefully, probing with an occasional question. It felt like the old days when we would play backgammon. I would play to beat him; he would play to discover who I was.

He seemed to derive vigor from our conversation; his ashen face looked several shades better. He told me one might come to believe that mixing colors of oil paint creates art. That is how oils work; the mixing of primary colors creates all the others, all the layers. Paints always work that way. *It's a physical law.*

But that's not what creates the art.

I felt confused. He was ever the teacher, and perhaps I was reluctant to hear what he was saying.

"So, why is it that you're still seeking?" Had he changed the subject?

The answer to that was easy. "I'm not doing what I ought to be doing."

"I don't believe that's true. That would make life rather

silly, wouldn't it? Don't mistake where you are when the time comes to be somewhere else, not if you want to know peace." he said.

I was stunned. Didn't I have peace?

"No, you have ambition." Futzu said and then inserted, "Nothing wrong with ambition, unless, of course, you are compelled to be ambitious."

We fell silent.

Then Futzu added, wouldn't I like to see a grizzly bear?

Sure, love to, furthest thing from my mind.

I looked over at him as I drove. He was serious.

He told me he'd like to see one, too, if I would oblige by exercising a bit of that *law of attraction*. Then he started looking at the moving landscape as if one might suddenly appear.

I never could get used to his abrupt changes.

Grizzlies were plentiful here in Alaska; I knew that. But I wasn't as naive as to suppose we were just going to drive down any road and meet a brown bear. Perhaps we could see one hiking, or on a stream stacked with salmon running, but not from a car window. And Futzu obviously wasn't going to be leaving the car.

"Okay," he said, "go into that pullout there," which I did. That's when the he closed his eyes in obvious and sustained pain.

Futzu eventually opened his eyes and bantered with me. "Go on then. I guess I'll have to stay in the car this time." The fact that he was dying of cancer didn't seem to enter into anything.

I smiled uncomfortably at him and stepped out. I'd never been North before, but I quickly realized that wilderness could start three feet from a road up here in Alaska. I was a desert rat, clearly out of my element. Before me lay concentrated every hue of green the universe could produce, gathered into one majestic sweep. I took a few steps from the gravel pullout into the larger world. The muskeg floor was spongy with untold depths of lichen, moss, and netted roots. This floor swept down a valley scattered with distant beds of purple blossoming fireweed, a shock of color in what was otherwise a sea of green.

The lush valley was bordered with timber, rich, untouched logging potential, and glaciated peaks glimmering in the rare clear summer sky. At the bottom of the valley ran a tremendous river, more like the width of a lake for a desert dweller. It was oddly colored in grays and azure, since it was heavily laden with glacial silt.

I didn't know this huge river had been flowing for only a few weeks, the few weeks since the winter breakup, and would be freezing solid again in a several weeks more. How could I have appreciated how short the season of life was in this place, since so far I'd experienced only a slice of it? It was 10:30 at night, but it still felt like the early evening. That was the power of distortion this far north.

Gorgeous view, but no brown bear. The way Futzu brought up the subject, I'd almost expected to step out of the car and shake paws with one.

I looked back at the car. Francis's eyes were closed again.

I decided, why not? I'll bite. Closing my eyes, I imagined a bear. In my mind, it was before me on all four legs. The animal looked at me, twisting its nose east and then west, testing the air. My own breath was heavy with the scent of its musk. Then it stood to tower above me, a 12-foot giant, and roared at the sky. Claws capable of shredding caribou reached toward me. So real was my imagining, I took a step back from the apparition.

A pickup truck, dragging an overlarge RV, drove into the pullout from the direction we were headed. It blocked my rental car from sight. Out popped a couple of Alaskan Highway travelers.

"Hello."

"Hello."

"What a day," said one middle-aged man. "This is a nice change from the rain."

I nodded and made to go past him.

"There's a moose around the corner back there, on the south side, in the water," the traveler said.

I thanked him for the uninvited information and walked back to my car.

Futzu opened his eyes. "Well?" he asked. I shook my head, smiling down at my lap, and told him there was no bear, but the tourist had mentioned a moose down the road.

"Ah, of course," said Futzu. "We're supposed to see a

moose." I smiled again and started the engine. All of a sudden, I was having fun. It was indeed around the next curve, in a pond. Not a very impressive moose. I'd expected a gargantuan bull with a huge rack. Instead we got this small, pleasant female placidly chewing on a lily pad.

Futzu took endless delight in watching it. He commented that it was fine, though it wasn't a bear. His tone could have been construed as a parental scolding. He looked at me and asked, "What's holding you up?" Then he prodded me again. "I asked you for a Kodiak, instead got moose." Somehow he had gotten me caught up in this game, and now I was having trouble making a reality check. I'd flown 4,000 miles to visit my dying mentor of 20 years ago and he had me out looking for a damn bear.

He looked bad, but not like not death, not like he had when I first saw him in bed. But I could tell his body was using every ounce of energy to be in this excursion away from his B&B, which was now several miles back. This was unrealistic.

"Why did you ask me to come here, Francis? What is it you want?" It came out.

"Why, nothing. I have everything I want. What do you want?"

I smiled sardonically. Same old Futzu. "I guess I want to see a brown bear."

"Thought so," replied Francis. We moved down the road.

"What are you waiting for?" Futzu asked me as we drove in the endless evening. The man had a gift for opening

Pandora's box.

"I'm not waiting. I'm doing everything I know to do. Life's a process, isn't it? Enjoy the process, right?" I replied. "I can't relax, though. I'm not doing what I was born to do."

"No." Futzu shook his ashen face tiredly, but his eyes were lively. "What are you waiting for, as in, the sooner you find the bear, the sooner I get back to bed." He coughed and missed wiping the phlegm from his chin.

Oh, that's random as hell. I became angry at this sport.

"Right! I can't just stop the car anywhere, walk behind any tree and say hello grizzly bear."

Francis looked at me with tired patience. "Why not?" he asked.

Fine! I hit the brakes and pulled off to the shoulder. I slammed the car door and took a few steps into the trees.

This was silly. I didn't find a thing. Biting flies found me. One took a hunk out of my arm and made it run with blood. I smashed it in defense and returned to the driver's seat.

I sat there for a spell. "It doesn't work like that," I told Futzu.

"Of course not. Who said it did?" he answered.

"I don't know," I said. "Is this really what you want to do, why I traveled all this way?"

"Yes, please." Futzu coughed again. A slightly septic smell rose from him.

"I just can't produce a bear so you can go back to bed."

"Why not?" he asked again.

"I guess I'm not ready," I said.

"Oh, you're ready."

"Then I'm not capable."

"Wrong again."

"I don't believe this."

"Bingo," he said.

"Look, I don't have to miraculously manifest a Kodiak bear, out of the blue, to prove the law of attraction. And just because I can't doesn't mean I don't create. I've never seen anyone materialize something in that way, so that mustn't be what creating is about."

"Right! I'm glad we got that straight. So what is it all about?" he said.

"*I don't know!*" I exclaimed.

"So why waste my time trying to see a bear?"

I wanted to scream. Could he possibly be more opaque?

His face became mild and reassuring. "Well then, where I want to go is coming up in about four more miles. I appreciate this favor," he said. His breathing was labored. We drove in silence.

Futzu had me position the car so that upon opening his door he could see both the historical marker and the mountain peak it referenced in the same view.

The sign described how the peak was named after a young lieutenant given the mission to create a trail joining some coast to some inland corridor. It was a scenic spot and an impressive peak. But this was Alaska, and I was already realizing the scene was a dime a dozen. I wondered why this particular spot was important to Francis. He sat exhausted but pleased, smiling, and took it in.

The range and the peak were above tree line. It was white topped but didn't have a glacier, nothing spectacular by northern standards. Yet he only had eyes for this. Living so close, I'm sure, he'd seen this hundreds of times.

"It's my circle," he started to explain, perhaps sensing my curiosity. "It's a gift to be connected to one's past."

"How does this connect you to your past?"

He didn't answer, just smiled and looked on. "I've always known our connection, too, Hoch San, and the agreements we made to each other long before we met." I thought about that, and somehow it made sense to something deep within me, and I began to detect what was happening. This was the part of creation that always set me back, reignited my fear. It was the aspect I most needed to master, the part where nothing was so permanent as never to change. I could smell endings everywhere around me. The terra firma I had elaborately acquired in life was falling away once again as I quaked with uncertainty.

"A journey of a thousand miles begins with a list, Hoch San," he said to me. "Make a list, gather what you need, and go. What are you waiting for?"

The dusk was finally catching up with us in this land of the midnight sun. I honored Futzu's request to dwell. He watched as the peak fell into darkness.

I had a place like this; it was in the desert Southwest, a place I recognized the first time I'd laid my eyes on it. In no way that reasoning could justify, I knew the place as home. No matter how many times I returned, my heart danced when I saw it, and all the roads of all my journeys connected me to there. I knew what the hoodoos meant, knew their story, felt what the old ones felt, and understood the heart of the ravens. All this that I knew, I had no way to know. Therefore, I told no one.

So I watched the young lieutenant's and my Futzu's mountain from the hood of the rental car for what seemed like all eternity, remembering my ancient canyon home and feeling a sense of peace restored.

Finally I slid from the hood and rounded the passenger door to see if he was ready to go. His gaze was locked on the peak there in the darkness. His eyes were open but without life. Futzu had already gone.

I drove Francis home for his last time, with deep respect, back to the B&B. At one point on the drive, my headlights caught a massive animal walking beside the road. It was large like a buffalo but dish-faced and hump-shouldered, a regal predator. I barely noticed it in this holy of all moments. It wasn't exactly when imagined or exactly as imagined, but it didn't matter. That wasn't what it was about, at least not anymore.

Trip List

The normal pattern of rain and summer chill returned to the Alaskan summer. I stayed two days with Nora. The night before leaving, I was alone in the common room for hours, sipping brandy and warming myself by the fire. Futzu had reminded me, "A journey of a thousand miles begins with a first step." And for me, he meant a trip list.

I sat down and wrote quietly. I had never gotten around to describing succinctly what I wanted. What it was, exactly, that made me ever so restless.

I started by writing down all my desires, without worrying about how to accomplish them. After I had scribbled out several pages of pretty great stuff, I wadded them up and chucked them into the fire.

I had a new inspiration. There was a simpler way. I divided a sheet of paper into two halves. The left side would be the list of things I should do. On the right I would write down the things to leave to the universe.

Then I stalled and stared into the hearth. I was drawn deep into the burning embers, how the glowing hardwoods continuously opened and burst with energy as they transformed. Flames danced and bedazzled with uncontrived delight.

Mankind has gazed into fire for eons, attempting to understand its simple mystery. Fire captivates us, but ever we miss the connection. Here was true magic, and all it took was a single match to ignite it. Then the blaze sustained itself. After striking it, there was nothing left but to sit back and receive the warmth. Properly laid fires just take off. One doesn't need to empty a whole matchbox of affirmations into them.

The time had come when I no longer wanted control. I pared my desires to five things and placed each of them on the universe's side of the list:

Abundant funding.

That spells freedom, enough to share, enough to explore, and the zeal to do it.

Okay then, freedom for what?

Discover and practice what I came here for.

I'm not sure of the whole of this, but I know its parts, for they tug on me.

Travel, explore, share.

There are many places that beckon to me. I've often thought it would be great to live three months at a time in these places, in their cultures, long enough to absorb them and let them operate on me, and I on them. Then capture all that in a way I can share it with others, in a way that excites life.

Good so far. Now how should I feel? That's easy.

Joy. What else is there?

And now for the coup de grace. It was time to jot down a purpose.

Here's the rub, I thought. I'm a bit uncompassionate. I admit that. I know all too well that it wouldn't help to join those around me who suffer, but at the same time I too easily dismiss them. Worse yet, sometimes I'll offer a few observations on how they cause their misery and how they might correct it. Even if I'm right, and that's beside the point, this still makes me a brute.

True compassion leads to something alien and reluctant, full of qualities unknown that I lack. So I added this last item to the list.

Become loving. Serve.

I wasn't sure what this might come to mean. But Francis's last act was to serve me. *The student serves the master, the master serves all.*

I set the list aside and watched the fire until it burned itself out. I never looked at that list again. It wasn't necessary. It was completed; all three levels of me were in agreement.

Looking back now, I realize it was the last entry on the list that was the source of all subsequent havoc.

WATCH FOR FALLING ROCKS

I had the wrong vehicle for the journey of that list. Turns out I needed wings, not wheels, because there was a chasm between me and what I needed. However, since I had just the one vehicle and deemed it sturdy, there was no choice but to floor the accelerator and try to jump the gulf.

Six months after returning from Alaska, my business partner and close friend betrayed me. At least it felt like betrayal at the time. He sat across a table telling me, quite out of the blue, that our business and our friendship were hereby terminated without notice. He was going it alone and snatching our livelihood for himself while he was at it. He didn't give a damn how I made a living. I decided that this outcome had little to do with me. He'd always led a dramatic and painful existence that made everything a burden; though he had a brilliant mind and an earnest soul, he was ever brutalized by his dreadful choices in matters of the heart. Nonetheless, he might as well be saying, this limb of ours that reaches for success, I amputate.

So I bled out. Mostly, I felt terrified facing the end of the enterprise I'd given nearly everything to create. I had thought it was going to be the source of my abundant funding; now it was going to leave me destitute. I'd never known more stress. The hull of my vessel was buckling under the pressure.

Ellen, who was always there, was there for me as I agonized. At first she tolerated my outrage at my friend and business partner. I poured out an endless diatribe of "blame" and "unfair," with excruciating details of "unappreciated" and "immoral," while she patiently poured me coffee. In my tirade, I also re-tread some complaints I had about the way she managed things in her life, things that always ended up on my shoulders. She stopped pouring coffee.

I had touched on that theme of *Ellen disapproval,* the one I'd been absently working on for years. I finally noticed what I'd been doing, for so long, to my most important relationship. There were places in Ellen's heart that had shut their doors to me. It had been an act of self-preservation, of survival. They had been shut for quite some time; I just hadn't recognized it.

How many others in my life were there upon whom I had trodden?

Wrecked at the bottom of a chasm, one I was never meant to leap across, I searched desperately for the way out.

I recall sitting alone in my mountain house, days after those events had exploded into my life. Winter's gray light was pouring through tall windows situated on either side of our empty fireplace. Bone-cold air sneaked in through the chimney damper. An ice storm was slashing the far hillside across from our land, obscuring juniper trees.

I was reflecting on the last item on my list—*become loving*. That's the one I'd crashed upon. But now I clung to that entry above all else, especially in light of how my relations were tumbling around me. *Become loving.*

At that moment, all creation felt suddenly hollow. If you want a red truck, I thought, imagine it and expect it. It will make its way to your driveway, assuredly. That is law! But this law applies mindlessly to everyone, at all times, as unselective as gravity. It turns out that one can attract success and great possession or become a renowned artisan and still muck around with terrible lack.

I was beginning to understand that creation was a road, not a destination, and as much as I enjoy the road, I wouldn't want to be *forever* upon it. I love the road for the places it takes me.

The winter storm outside was in full regalia. Our high-ceilinged living room, built for solar gain, was always a bit cold in weather like this. Usually, Ellen and I built a fire to take the edge off the chill. But Ellen wasn't around, and I had no heart for it.

So I sat, uncomfortable and cold, on the couch, thinking how the road I was set upon was leading me to arrive alone. Ellen was turning away, and my business partner found no solace in me. I'd been a magnet to others due to my creativity and zeal, but also kept everyone at arm's length. I'd become content in life. I was happy with myself and by myself. But it was contentment born from playing it safe, isolating my feelings from others and learning not to worry overly much about theirs.

Can't create for somebody else, I'd concluded—ergo, everyone take care of yourself! Along with that, I'd developed a notion that I'd never feel regret.

As I gazed through the cold windows, childhood memories made a tight circle around me, like old classmates at the bus stop pressing in and hollering while an overly tall juvenile made good on his promise to annihilate me after school. I put arms over my head and curled up on the ground so his fists mostly glanced off. Only a few of his blows really hurt, but they all did real damage. By now, Mom hardly ever asked. I stopped telling her; she stopped checking.

I detested what I saw reflected in the glass of my parent's porch window. I wished I could change that image, look like my older brother. Instead I saw only the ugliness the other children made me feel. "No, son, you're a handsome young man," Daddy said and, believing he'd helped, turned back to his gardening, having no idea how deep it went. No friends, not ever. Everyone distant and inaccessible, too often cruel. And I—I was a pariah, desperately alone, better off alone. Were it possible, I would've changed. But I had no clue how to be what they wanted, to be someone else. My indoctrination into this world went poorly.

As I recollected my past, the beliefs of that wretched child poured in to bite at my heart. My family was of modest means, unable to afford the things I wanted. There simply wasn't enough in the world to go around, little left for me. I started stealing small things. I might try to occasionally cheat this lack, but mostly I'd do without. I was ever without as I hid within.

I blinked in the drab light of our living room, banishing that long-gone child back to his painful past. That version of me no longer existed. I had exorcised it long ago. Hadn't I?

I'm so sorry, Ellen, I thought as I peered through cold glass at the frozen world. Perhaps there's room for regret after all.

Easy transitions? I guess not.

I was now being violently disassembled in order to be re-made. And as brutal as the process might turn out to be, I chose to embrace it, though with much trepidation about what might loom next on the horizon.

The freezing storm raged outside my window, layering ice on the forest's trees, which now bent under their new burden. My eyes traveled from the storm to the empty fireplace. A collection of spiritual self-help books had been accumulating on shelves above our mantel. I walked over to the mantel and started browsing through their titles. All of them had left out mention of this aspect of the journey.

I carefully stacked all the books in the fireplace and turned them into a jolly bonfire. There I roasted marshmallows over them in solitude. Because, when all else fails, I'm still fond of roasted marshmallows.

Demons & Car Payments

Eighteen months after composing my list, magic had all but left the world. I was eyeball to eyeball with limitations I couldn't see. Reality had congealed into a stubborn mass as I found myself traveling the same road, around and around.

Futzu once told a story I'd never fully understood, of a faithful student whose heart was blown wide open with enlightenment at the moment he finally recognized his surroundings. He rejoiced, screaming to his teacher, "Master, I see it all clearly now—I've been here before!" With that, his master struck him violently to the ground, asking, "How many times?"

I decided not to tell Ellen I was facing financial ruin. The dry spell had been longer this time than ever before, and a sparkling new calamity had just arrived; this after so much had fallen into my lap. All of a sudden, I could see nothing on the horizon. I was losing my will to press on, alone in this business enterprise that my friend and partner had abandoned.

God damn you, Garrit; you screwed me.

The instant that flared in my head, I retracted it.

No, Garrit, I won't feel that way. I realize you had to.
I actually did.

The dark prospect of working for someone else was one of the major fears I'd faced a year ago, sitting in our combined office as the front door bounced hard and failed to reseal on its magnetic security lock because Garrit had banged it so furiously on his way out.

I hadn't seen my partner like that in all our 17 years. It was a perverted side of him I couldn't believe existed, surfaced from nowhere to breathe air and fire. The pressure in his soul must have been unimaginable. They say no one really changes, but there it was. When the breaking point allowed his demon to take control, he was unrecognizable. It was scary, and I was shaken.

I recall gazing blankly at the list of design tasks we always kept in erasable ink on the white board. Next to the list was the diagram of a driver circuit we had brainstormed together not a month earlier.

His rage was still echoing off the fluorescent-bathed office walls.

"I was designing electronics before you were in high school, and you can *GO TO HELL!*" Those were his last wild-eyed words. His chair, which had crashed on the floor as he pounded up from the table, was still rocking, though he was gone.

Crazy! I sat there stunned. The Corporate Opportunity Act lay untouched on the table. I was only halfway through my proposal. Our business lawyer said Garrit couldn't legally take our design customers and form his own business, not unless I agreed. I left out the part where our lawyer said I could garnish half his money if he did.

But I was about to tell him I would grant him permission, sign away my rights. Even in this ruination, I wanted to allow his choice. I would remember who he was, even if, for the time being, he'd forgotten.

Before I could tell him what I had in mind, my reasonable friend left his body. In his place appeared a desperado who justified eradicating me if it meant his survival.

With a shaking hand, I lifted my office mug and sipped on cold coffee.

He had been unusually dark of late, but I had endured it. Maybe I should've been prepared from the moment I met him; this extraordinary genius functioned rather poorly in our world after all. The first time I was introduced to him, he actually ignored me for a half-hour, leaving me standing at his back while he worked at his computer screen. Then he blinked in genuine surprise when he discovered that I might find this discourteous.

Now our office had never felt so barren. My eyes traveled to a hole in the carpet. Filthy dull carpet, ragged, unattended, and snarled fibers jeered at me. It was like seeing that 10-year-old tear for the first time, and suddenly I couldn't bear it.

So I stood and wandered into the lab. The lab was in its usual state of disarray. Previous projects lay piled up, with just enough space cleared for the current one. Garrit was disorderly and abhorred cleaning up after an exhausting job, and I abhorred cleaning up by myself. So there the messes sat, as they almost always did.

I leaned against the lab door. I hadn't seen his breaking point coming. Perhaps I should've paid more attention several months ago when he announced that our office was now a *sanctuary* from his troubles; we'd no longer spend the morning hours talking through his woes. Selfishly, I agreed. That sounded like a good idea. Over the years, it had worn on me. But who in this entire world would that leave for him to talk to?

He snapped during our extreme business downturn. For the first time, we'd been living off our personal savings for months. Even though he was 12 years my senior, he probably had little savings to speak of. It was likely he didn't have the means to retire. His fifth wife had put the finishing touches on his financial demise, and his current wife was causing him unrelenting misery.

Six wives! How could I have expected someone so dysfunctional in all other relationships to succeed with ours? I kept our friendship alive by pardoning your arrogant oddities, Garrit, and you always took more than you gave. How dare you become offended at me? I carried you all those years when you could barely work, during your divorces—

Stop, David!

I struggled to shake off that toxic explosion of blame. I

knew, deep down, it was all too convenient to fault him.

I, too, was under a breaking force. However, I was better prepared since I'd summoned change—with my list. I had commanded the universe to move, and move it had—even if not as expected. I hadn't known Garrit needed to move as well. So be it, he was part of this. But for me, there was a stable home and relationships to help me through the storm. He had no port.

I decided to stop sipping cold coffee from my mug and wandered to the kitchen area, where I refreshed it.

Another mess lay in this area, ignored like all the others.

The meeting I set up with him today didn't go at all like I'd planned. Ever since he delivered his edict to terminate us, an evil brew had settled in my heart. But as I woke this morning, things looked up. I had a new inspiration. Something told me to let my friend go, stop feeling angry at him—to take over the business myself.

"Impossible" had been my knee-jerk response. I can't cover his skill set. Besides, the company is flat broke.

Trust, responded the whatever guidance.

I noticed that my hand had a wet paper towel in it and was idly wiping at stains on the kitchen-area counter. Even though Garrit blew up in my face, I was opting to trust the original inspiration. I would complete for us what we couldn't complete together.

That was the idea on the day he left. Then after spending the next year doing it, everything that followed indicated it was the right idea. Four quarters' worth of orders materialized from nowhere. The business was magically funded. New representatives dropped from nowhere to take us to the next level in Silicon Valley. The doors had reopened, and the gold was flowing.

That year went by filled with quiet determination.

But then once again I found myself sitting alone in the office. Everything had come to an end, and I was once more staring at the carpet, brand-new blue carpet this time. The lab behind me was meticulously organized and spotless. A project was there on the bench, just one of many I had learned to solo, absent the synergism of my partner.

The dry spell was the longest ever; nothing from the Silicon Valley reps, nothing from the new market, nothing from any corner. To make matters worse, the customer I had risked one-third of my bank account for had just got off the phone. "Not interested after all!"

I'm in real trouble.

I trembled yet again in the face of the unknown. Is there no such thing as security? I twisted in the black office chair, spinning with stress. Here I was, trapped among familiar but deadly fears—I've been here before.

"How many times?" asked the master as he struck his student to the ground. ... The philosophy slammed into my head.

I've been here *before*?

—*I've been here before.*

After all these years, it finally clicked. I silently thanked Francis for a gift he'd buried as a time capsule along my path.

The faithful student in Futzu's story had thought enlightenment would change his life—not so.

And like the master from the story, my universe had struck a violent blow to wake me up and get me moving—prevent me from becoming stuck, reveling in awareness. It provided this perfect storm to expose my missteps so I might correct course.

But nothing would change until I took hold of the rudder, to steer in a direction consistent with those lofty requests I'd made and placed on a list—take action, practice navigating, ... polish my mirror.

I knew, at that moment, that I was forever ensnared by what I considered secure in life, by the observable. I must embrace this unknown instead of fearing it. Out of the fog of the unknown the greatest ships have come to harbor, and I've always been given safe passage.

Perhaps someday I'd thank Garrit for kicking us from the cradle and parading out the host of demons possessed by me, not the least of which was the demon of lack.

I decided again not to tell Ellen I was facing financial ruin, because she would laugh at me, telling me I said the same thing every spring. She's so much more in touch with abundance than I am. She doesn't worry.

And I didn't want her to laugh at me. Not this time. I'd rather find a way to laugh at myself.

Parable under the Hood

The exploding sound came from somewhere to the left and above.

"What was that?" The engine was suddenly on edge, where it had been purring an instant before.

The sound detonated again.

Every component on the front of the engine heard it, and everything from the engine backward felt the shock waves.

The alternator winced. Somewhere deep in its coils it knew what was behind the violent sound. Something like this had happened before, and there remained deep gashes in the alternator's casing from that last time. Those slices through its casing had never been repaired and had never completely bandaged over with grime either. So moisture and other environmental troubles slowly seeped in, hurting the delicate parts of the alternator's workings. It was undeserved.

The compressor for the air conditioner was about to go critical once again and bring the whole world under the hood to the brink.

How could the alternator not take it personally, given the history it had with the AC compressor? It would have loved to move to a different part of the engine if it could, disavow any relation with the AC. That turned out to be impossible. To make matters worse, they were on the same fan belt and, therefore, forever had to deal with each other as relatives.

The compressor had a defect that no one knew about. It was cocked in its mount. Perhaps that had been true since original assembly; perhaps it happened during some trauma early in life.

Misaligned it was, though, regardless of the cause. This probably led to the dysfunctional family of parts immediately attached to the compressor. For instance, the compressor's mate, the freewheeling pulley, had been supportive and good for it originally. But the twist in the compressor's alignment put unfair stress on the freewheeling pulley, and over time the pulley began to screech.

Now it screeched constantly at the compressor, so incessantly that the compressor wanted the nag to be removed at any cost. Together they now created a horrible vibration that stressed and began to crack the umbilical attachment they had to their pride and joy, the hose that transported the precious coolant. The coolant was the focus of their existence, and it was beginning to seep out the cracks and flee from them into the atmosphere.

The compressor was the highest-dollar and the highest-maintenance accessory under the hood and damn well wanted everything else to appreciate it. After all, it kept the vehicle's passengers comfortable in the desert. It was indispensable. It also resented the load the little alternator put on their shared fan belt, especially when it was hot outside and the compressor had hard work to do. It thought the alternator should be more respectful, more impressed, and certainly more helpful. Why couldn't the alternator occasionally help out by cooling the cabin, too?

But no, the alternator was too preoccupied with its self-centered task of providing electrical power to everything. Worse yet, the alternator could pretty much ignore the compressor, since no current, on any wire, flowed from its generator coils to the AC compressor. This, of course, made the compressor all the more bent.

As far as the AC compressor was concerned, the alternator was plain selfish. The alternator laid its values of electricity on everything else in the engine. The compressor had invited the alternator on numerous occasions to cool events, but the alternator rarely responded. In fact, if it did attend, the alternator just brought its stupid electricity.

By now the twist in the mount of the compressor made everything in its guts hurt, its axle bowed, and its seals wore. To the compressor, the pain seemed to originate from the clutch pulley on its nose. Like everything else along its axis, it was misaligned. So the fan belt that spun the clutch on the compressor's nose relentlessly ground shards into the compressor's raw internal wounds. By easy association, the compressor pretty much decided that all this was the alternator's fault, since the alternator was the one constantly tugging on that fan belt.

The last time the compressor's clutch failed and froze, the resulting friction overheated and then quickly severed their shared rotating belt. The compressor sent the high-rpm belt whiplashing across the front of the engine and nailed the alternator squarely in its casing. There was no telling if the compressor felt better for having lashed out at the alternator, but the harm it was capable of was now clear.

The owner replaced the frozen clutch and, in apparent deference to the compressor, threw away the screeching freewheeling pulley. But the owner missed the defect in the AC compressor's mount, leaving the compressor as torqued as ever. Divorced from the freewheeling pulley, the shriek was gone. However, matters were due to get worse. The compressor now had to operate without any spousal support to offset the pressure from the relentless strain of the fan belt.

However, the inevitable blowup was a bit delayed. During the repair, the compressor, attempting to feel better about existence, started to practice existentialism. It became acquainted with shop manuals that gave insight into the inner mechanical spirit, the magic of operational life, and the power of repair. It started to think, among other things, that it could heal itself by not believing in mounting problems.

In line with its newfound center and understanding of inner workings, it became the mechanical spiritual sage of the engine. The compressor sent a long message to the alternator, explaining, "It doesn't seem to occur to you that your values of providing electricity aren't the same as my values of cooling. Perhaps you don't share the values of anything else in the engine, for that matter. And you don't bother to ask."

The compressor went on to explain how its own good-hearted tolerance of the alternator frequently put the compressor in the position of not acknowledging its own cooling desires. The compressor told the alternator that it was surprised at how incredibly unevolved and self-interested the alternator was. Not that this was wrong. It was ... just what it was.

From its higher spiritual plane, the compressor added that it was delivering this message in detachment and as a spiritual service so that the alternator might learn and grow from the mechanical life lesson. The compressor continued by suggesting that if the alternator ever really wanted to seek a meaningful relationship in cooling, the compressor would be there.

"Should you ever decide that's *something of value* to you."

The message ended with the words "I bow to the struggles, learnings, and joys of your inner spirit in this mechanical existence."

Poor alternator was confused. Was the compressor correct? Somehow, as elevated and spiritually evolved as the message was, it still felt bad. Alternator was a bit defensive. After all, didn't the alternator provide power to the fans that blew air through the compressor's coolant pipes and onto the vehicle's passengers? So, as far as the alternator was concerned, it played some role in cooling. Come to think of it, there wouldn't be any cooling without the amperage it provided to those fans.

It knew the compressor would never see it that way, though. The alternator was ready to give up on the relationship with the compressor. The alternator was beginning to realize it would only ever be what the compressor saw it as. The alternator just wanted to go on with its existence, find a way to ignore the expectations of that troubled compressor it was joined to.

So that's precisely what the alternator did—purposefully ignored it and left the compressor to its newfound enlightenment, deciding the compressor wasn't that vital to the alternator anyway.

The alternator ignored its interconnection to the compressor for almost a thousand miles until the moment when the explosion in the compressor occurred. The explosion was so severe that it took out the entire front workings on the engine. The alternator was murdered immediately, which killed the power to the spark plugs. This, of course, made the engine die. Since the vehicle was traveling at high speeds, the operator lost control, and so, too, did the whole vehicle's world come to an end.

Don't Let Anyone Pass You

Ellen's tears were streaming down her red, flaring cheeks, and now she spoke more quickly between sobs. I watched her from across the two-person jet bath as she used the back of her bent hands to mop the streams from her pooling eyes. Part of me was still angry, part childishly stubborn, and part falling in love all over again with those elegant bends in her wrists. Mostly, I was cursing myself.

How had I let this happen *again*? Every war we'd ever known started the moment I became offended. If only I could stop taking things personally. This wasn't about me—even if she *was* biting my head off.

The shadow had crossed Ellen's soul once again. Perhaps it was genetic, perhaps some subtle chemical imbalance. Given that alcoholic parents had devoured her family, I'd always assumed it had more to do with circumstance. Most of Ellen's days were pleasant enough, preoccupied with the kids, work, or managed with amusing diversions. We did our best to sidestep her frequent outbursts. Healing touches from my hands applied nightly in the form of back rubs helped immensely. There were happy times, but darkness ever loomed. On occasion, she would awaken to utter emptiness.

She and I dealt with her depression in separate ways. I glazed over and, offering a handful of lame solutions, dispatched her to find happiness. She lashed out at the only person she'd ever dared to let that close: me.

This morning, yet again, I missed the message encrypted in her heated words and lost the opportunity to do some actual good. Instead, I took it personally and pulled out my broadsword to decapitate that poisonous attack.

She became so frustrated with my poor responses that she said, "Everything's all about you. Isn't it? You're completely useless. Selfish bastard!" Even as my heart silently screamed, *No! That's not me*, some frailty, somewhere deep inside, agreed, accepted the toxin, and trapped me in a dream of hell. From that instant, I was in a fight for my life, and I wholly missed her plea for help. What would it take for me to change? I frantically searched my tapes for anything that would lead back to the pleasant beginnings of our bath. But I knew it was too late. I knew Ellen. It was going to be a while before she trusted me again.

The simple truth is, as stubborn as we both are, and as inappropriate as we might become, she never really hurts me. I suppose that's because of her nature, and my knowledge of it. She can strike out viciously, and I detest that. But it has no roots and blows away at the end of the scene.

I do hurt her, though, time and again. I know that now, probably always did, but I'd always been too focused on me to pay enough attention. I hurt her because of the ways I disapprove of her, and her heart knows it. She recoils in shock at the unlovingness. Now that I was seeing it, as if for the first time, it was killing me.

I wanted to reach out, take her small hand, and say I didn't mean it. It wasn't that important. Ask if she could see how much progress I've made overall. Tell her my unchecked outrage wasn't so noteworthy. It's just a habit, really, another bad habit that I'm quitting.

I didn't try to take her hand. I knew she would've just snatched it away. I sat there in the bubbling water watching Ellen's graceful curves as they curled up. Her back was to me now. I was completely miserable.

I pushed that ancient memory out of my mind as Ellen and I traveled Combs Ridge toward the town of Bluff and away from the tall spires that had two days ago produced my climbing disaster. Something told me I was doing a lot of that on this hastily taken trip, pushing out of my mind. I also knew, for the present, it was the right thing to do. It had now been three years since I first composed my list. Ellen and I had healed many of our self-inflicted wounds, and I loved her more than I ever thought possible. I put my hand on her hip as she slept.

Combs Ridge rose ahead of us like a giant tsunami, a gargantuan wave made of sandstone, geologically locked at the point where the crest was foaming to break, with white Navajo-sandstone tops and red underbelly catching the sunset light.

This Land's End was one of two sheer walled cliff barriers that marched across the horizons. The other, somewhat behind me, was the Mokee Dugway. Together they formed a thousand-foot-tall walled confinement that separated the upper table of the ancestral puebloan's land from the floor of the Navajo Monuments, which I was leaving.

A passage had been blasted out of Combs Ridge for man's road decades ago. Row above row of dynamite drill holes oddly decorated the tall wall faces for as high up as could be seen and marched like petroglyph fence posts in front of me. As I passed through, I was dazzled once again by the engineering feat of the passageway. The ingenuity it took to carve this mammoth notch in the natural barrier has been taken for granted, I thought; our mastery over an immovable mountain of rock. "They will say to the mountain, 'Move from here!' and it will move."

Others might criticize this as a scar and claim man has desecrated nature. I have too often heard mankind referred to in this manner, as if we were an aberration, apart from and an enemy to the natural world.

Nonsense!

Man is nature's ultimate masterpiece and favorite child, as far as I was concerned. I was in awe of humans capable of creating a dramatic passage through living stone and driving through in a machine so wondrous and complex that no single soul could possess the totality of knowledge, craft, or art contained therein.

It was true that a noxious mix of gases pumped out the rear of the auto and that man could go too far with his dynamite. But this was wholly natural, in my observations, as nature itself often goes too far of its own accord. I've come across desert pothole ponds bloated with the bodies of tadpoles that annihilated themselves because their multiplying numbers polluted their world into extinction. I've seen piñon forests die across four states because the temporary advantage of drought was exploited by beetles that ordinarily harvest only diseased trees, then watched as fire in these standing dead forests took everything.

I wouldn't expect a tadpole, a piñon beetle, or fire to think of moderating itself for the good of the environment. Only mankind has the sentiment to do that; mankind, nature's golden children. I guarantee that time will naturally pound and erode the Mokee Dugway, and this beautiful Combs Ridge, into rubble. The nature of man merely eroded a notch out of it ahead of the nature of wind, ice, heat, and rain; in this case, a rather useful erosion.

Time was running out, and time with Ellen was precious on this trip. I didn't want it to end. Once again, and all the more, I couldn't stand the thought of driving home. I had to sustain this excursion and prolong it.

The sign to Sand Island might as well have jumped into the middle of the road and planted itself there.

That's it! I braked, turned off the highway and headed for the campgrounds at Sand Island. My customers could wait some more. I was rather proud of not giving in, the way the responsible me demanded. It might stress the hell out of me later, but maybe not.

Still, there was something else. An unreasonable reluctance was mounting on this journey home, and it wasn't because I preferred the road. I don't know. It was way out of proportion. Something.

Anyway, I'd discuss the decision to camp another night with Ellen when she woke. Give her a chance to send us on home if she will. But I already suspected what her response would be. She's much less burdened by these matters than am I, and more spontaneous as a result.

So, I drove off the road, to spend another night camping in the redscape desert canyon, to join fitful nightmares that newly haunted me this trip but were forgotten before first light. The nightmares knew what in my mind was secret. They struggled alone against the knowledge that it was over—that now, I could never return home. They'd been screaming with dreadful images for five nights now as I slumbered. But their efforts to penetrate my conscious world were sabotaged because my mind erased the dreams before I awoke, winking each of them out. However, my mind could not entirely erase the unease left behind. Therefore, working through what lingered, my dreams masterfully needled me and laid their trap for me at Sand Island.

Unwittingly, I went to spend another endless night, longing for morning and Ellen's arms. And I went to Sand Island to mostly be sleepless in my sleeping bag for the sixth night in a row, strangely alone.

Pictures on the Wall

After parking the Land Cruiser in the choicest campsite, I walked back to the entrance. There I filled out an envelope at Sand Island's self-service fee station. It appeared we were the only campers tonight.

The path back to camp traveled beneath a tall bluff that was the reason for the location. I hopped over the broken-down 200-foot-long wooden fence that was originally erected to suggest a proper viewing distance. Picking my way along the bottom of the cliff, I navigated within a few feet of the extensively decorated wall.

There had to be a thousand pictographs on this rock face, each one with a special purpose and meaning that was lost to time.

As I walked, I thought about another decorated wall I often visited, similar to this one. That wall required a 39-mile hike down the gulch canyon system. It lay farther west, closer to the Colorado River. The gulch had experienced a minor Anasazi population boom for a few generations after the abandonment of the Chaco Great Houses and Mesa Verde Cliff Dwellings, somewhere around 1200 A.D.

The gulch's wall is one of three Ancestral Puebloan sites that my heart has recognized. Ellen has felt similar sensations there, and together we've conjectured unabashed about why this must be.

The pictographic wall at the gulch canyon is the length of a football field. Beneath its expansive ledge is a basin of piñon -lined meadows that had been *the gathering place.*

I can't prove this or explain how I know it. I identify those open fields as a result of some other experience.

The ancient basin had been a happy place. When hiking its perimeter, I sense campsites of different clans gathering in the slant yellow light after the season of harvest. The breeze echoes with games and kinship. The air transports the smell of fires and cooking food to me from across the ages, along with dog barks and turkeys squabbling underfoot.

On one occasion, Ellen had a dream in our tent as we camped on the basin floor. She woke me with amorous kisses, and we made love passionately on top of our sleeping bags. Afterward, Ellen told me how, in her dream, she had recalled the look of my Indian body lying next to hers in firelight.

The second place my heart knew was Moon House. My climbing buddy originally found this cliff dwelling and insisted I see it. He brought 150 feet of rope so we could rappel down the pour-off that denied access to the lower canyons below Moon House. This allowed us to make a circuit. That first expedition to the Moon House canyon was taken without Ellen because she was pregnant with our second child at the time.

To this day I remember dropping pack and climbing the reasonably accessible ledges under the cliff dwelling. Upon passing through the outer defensive wall, I saw above me the white full moon painted in a ceiling recess. It struck me with nostalgia, so thick with melancholy, that I fought tears.

The outer defensive wall did a remarkable job of preserving interior apartments eight centuries old. They still had roofs, still had interior benches and storage alcoves; and miraculously they all retained their mud-veneered exteriors. The walls of the inner apartments boasted a single line of white thumbprints stamped decoratively onto the adobe by the builders. That day, I placed my thumb into the print of a thumb almost a millennium gone, and my heart ached.

With my friend, I crawled through the grain-storage room at the far west end of this dark and compact cliff dwelling. Empty corncobs preserved by desert air for eight centuries were strewn on a floor deep with powdery dust. The granary's outside wall was gone, fallen down a 200-foot sheer drop, centuries ago.

My heart faltered when I saw what was beyond the missing wall, at the place where the cliff, which Moon House was built on, terminated. There rose three tall hoodoos, massive 50-foot spires of sandstone. Their shapes were humanlike, the heads of elders, forever on watch, looking up canyon.

Though I'd never seen it before, I knew that natural rock feature. It was the protectors, the reason Moon House was built on this particular cliff face. They protected me still. Three ancient fathers and mothers locked in stone, watching over me and my home while I was away.

The third and last place that felt familiar was this wall, here at Sand Island. This was not a gathering place, as in the gulch, but rather a place of passing for those journeying along the San Juan River. I slowly walked the wall, taking in each pictograph. These were the signs left along the Anasazi road.

I stopped at a set of two handprints. Hand paintings were of two styles: Outlined hands were created by painting ocher around outstretched fingers and a palm pressed against the rock; and solid hands were where the Anasazi stamped an imprint on the wall from a hand dipped in paint.

There were hundreds of these hands at various places along the wall, but this one un-extraordinary pair of handprints beckoned to me.

I held up my own hand, close to but not touching the smaller set, those of a youth, placed on this stone face alongside his father's as a rite of passage—far too long ago.

I closed my open hand and reached with a finger to touch the child's prints.

I felt remorse ... but didn't know why.

Crash

After setting up the tent at Sand Island, I paused to take in the dusk. The San Juan River thundered 20 feet from our campsite to the south, and the gentle bluffs to the north began to lose their scarlet color as the light diminished to black and white. In the east, I saw an arch of distended moon as it peeked over the horizon. At that same moment, the last rays of golden sun vanished in the west. The night in which the full moon would zenith was upon me.

I was weary. Tonight I looked at the red bluffs, and there was no heart in them. Gloom seeped from hidden places into my chest. I hadn't made any difference, I thought, as I surveyed the few familiar possessions I had brought and placed in this natural setting of lovely indifference.

All the colossal plans and vital things I wanted in life materialized to stand in judgment of me, and I was condemned. Among their court, I was surrounded by a magic moon rising, orange cast with sunset setting. I smelled fragrant sweet air left from a thunderstorm's passing rain, perfumed by wet desert sage. Drifting through piñon was the sound of a cactus wren harmonizing with a towhee's song. Everywhere was sweet comfort and warm-promise breeze. And all of them failed me. Life had gone out of them. It was a deceit that I had any control, just an attractive fiction that I'd believed in, too strong and too hard. Everything I thought mattered—has led to nowhere. I was lost.

At that moment I understood what makes a man old. I knew then how he begins to die when all the things he surrounded himself with no longer live for him. It was a daydream that fed and kept me, but now in nightfall's review, I've missed the target. I could let go now. It would've been better for me not to have aspired to so much in life. No expectations except, perhaps, some integrity and to love well. That would have been sufficient.

But now, preoccupied so long in the eternal foothills of strife, had I even loved well? Or had I forsaken it all while in pursuit of it all? So I saw, smelled, and tasted doubt, and submitted to an end, for I was weary. I was ready to close the book. The heart was gone from me as I turned toward the tent and prepared myself to be buried under six feet of slumber.

Yet, come the morn, was it burden or a grace that despair held no purchase on my heart after a night of sleep? When I woke I was surrounded by magic moon setting, orange cast with sun rising, air renewed in warm promising tones, birds flirting with me seductively from piñon, comfort given in stillness, and all of them fully summoned me.

They asked great and difficult things but gave them not up, since that was for me to divine.

Meeting Idiots at Rest Stops

*B*ink, *bink, bink, bink, bink,*
gerr-Thunk. Splash.

Seven.

This is too easy.

I hunted for a completely square rock to skip into the muddy San Juan, which was coursing through the Navajo sandstone formation walls. The roar from the white water slightly masked the sound my hiking boots made as I stumbled for footing on the bank's uneven surface.

Flat rocks skipped 12 times if thrown below the foaming Class III rapids, which was where I stood. With round rocks, I was getting at least seven, sometimes as many as nine before they buried themselves into the river.

Here's one that will be a challenge; it's shaped like a boot.

Bink, Thunk.

Two!

I'm an expert.

I was beginning to think I could skip a lead brick.

For the third time this morning, I reached and grabbed my right forearm with my left hand. I rolled the forearm while squeezing hard on the muscle, bone, and tendons. It didn't hurt. Only three days since it had been mangled under the boulder and it had recovered. My gut was pain-free, too. I was pleased by my body's recuperative powers.

What I should've been is downright astonished. If I'd had an X-ray for my arm and an MRI for my abdomen directly after the accident, I'd probably be more along the lines of frightened right now.

But no scientific evidence existed to show the original extent of my injuries, no diagnosis to explain that my hand shouldn't have been able to grasp an object, perhaps ever again. So I skipped rocks in blissful ignorance.

Okay, back to flat rocks. I'll try to skip one to the top of that canoe killer, pouring over a Volkswagen-size boulder.

The rock skipped over the tumultuous fore-water and buried itself in the pour-over with ease. Well done, I applauded myself.

It just takes practice, I thought as I reached for another flat stone. But I wasn't thinking about this semiprofessional sport of rock skipping. I was thinking about my business partner, my friend.

Forgiving him was not like turning off a light. Not as simple as "I forgive you." When pardoning him finally occurred to me, I thought that was all there was to it. I discovered I had a lot to learn about forgiving, especially forgiving someone who's not sorry.

Kerr-plop.

"Oops." Something must have affected my throw.

It was more like when I stopped smoking at the age of 27. Though I never lighted another cigarette, I was quitting for the next six years. I had to quit after every meal, a favorite part of the habit; quit with coffee, after making love, quit with this activity, that anxiety, over and over, each time any thread on the web of links to the habit was plucked. I had to develop tremendous fortitude and find ways to carry on when cravings became so strong that I could no longer remember why I was quitting in the first place. I had to practice quitting cigarettes a hundred times a day.

It seemed I'd had to practice forgiving my partner a hundred times an hour.

Whoops! I stopped the motion of my next throw. There actually *was* a canoe making its way to the head of the rapids. It was a Mad River model, maybe 16-foot, more than a match to the challenge if properly handled. My pulse rate elevated, as if I was in the bow or stern with the two paddlers.

They definitely were *not* setting up well for the huge pour-over, probably because its size obscured their view to the lower set of twin rapids that immediately followed. I was sure they had no idea of what was coming. They needed to enter the pour-over on the starboard side; they entered to the port.

Both were back-paddling on the approach, making the canoe all but stall in the heavy forward-churning current. On cue, both the stern man and the bow man started drawing their paddles in perfect unison at the exact same moment. They went neatly into the left chute. It was as impressive as could be; they were a good team. I stood on my toes, holding my breath for what was next, the part they hadn't anticipated.

The back-eddy from the downstream side of the juggernaut snapped their bow hard to the starboard.

"Crap!" They were immediately sideways to the next two rapids. That was the worst thing that could happen. Without realizing it, I had stepped into the river. Depending on what they did next, this could get dangerous in a hurry.

The T-bone collision with the rock hiding under the right-side rapid was inevitable, and it happened immediately. Pinned for a nanosecond! They had but one chance. If against all instincts they both leaned into the terrifying rapid instead of away from it and the bow man drew hard while the stern man power-stroked furiously, they might paddle off the tempest, and then only if they went to the right, not left, to avoid the other set of the twin rapids. With no time to think, those two would have to be practiced, gifted, and extremely lucky.

They didn't even make it to first base.

Caught off balance, one for certain and maybe both of them leaned away from the rapid instead of into it. The gunnels of the canoe that faced upstream dipped under the racing water, and that ended it. The canoe instantly filled with 200 gallons of water, scuttled, and vanished into the depths of white. I was now up to my knees in the river.

The paddlers were loose, on their own, and at the mercy of the furious current and unknown submerged dangers. The water below them crashed into itself and over rocks. It thundered under a perpetual mist created from its infinite collisions. With the application of velocity and constricted path, the normally soft, sustaining, and silky molecules of H_2O turned into a tortuous tree- and rock-crushing force.

The paddlers were wearing floatation devices, so they were washing through the field with heads above water, at least some of the time. Miraculously, their canoe avoided being pinned under from their miscalculation, for the tip of its bow somewhat surfaced a moment later, and it pinballed through the rapids. With amazing agility, one of the paddlers managed to rescue the canoe before the end of the rapids. He grabbed a gunnel but really just did his best to ride the current out and keep the boat alive.

The water beneath the rapids was still violent and the weight of the water-laden canoe, for someone treading in 8 or 10 feet of water, was too much for one. His partner was hopelessly separated, though, struggling to recover himself, and I could tell that guy was going to be lost for a while. He definitely had his own set of problems.

There was no way for me to help them without going for an exciting swim. Eventually, after an interminable quarter-mile or so, they teamed up again and labored to bring their swamped canoe near the bank, where they bailed it out, standing to their hips in water.

Been there, done that, I thought as I skipped another rock.

By now, I'd pretty much forgiven my partner. I knew this to be true because nowadays when I thought of him, I no longer had an emotional reaction. When I heard his name, it no longer hurt. If anything, I was beginning to recall fondness for him. I'd finally discovered the true power of forgiving him. I forgave him because I no longer wanted to continue paying for his injustice. It was me who needed to be freed from my outrage.

I watched as the canoers pulled their boat onto the riverbank and began reeling in the gear sacks that had been tied to the canoe with ropes. Then they sat next to each other on the bank, having what appeared to be a pensive conversation.

I could begin to see the good in the hideous and painful wipeout that my partner and I'd had. I now saw it as a gift. I was stronger, more aware of what I needed to do, closer to my goal than would have been possible if we'd continued on our course together. Our relationship had held me back.

I saw him more clearly, too, how hurting and in need of compassion he'd been. He'd been unwilling to talk to me in any personal way since his blowup. So I had no idea whether he ever thought to forgive me, but I prayed that he did.

By the time I was headed back to our Sand Island campsite, the water that soaked my pants to the knees had wicked up to my pockets and was heading for my crotch. So I wasn't in the mood to chat even though I immediately recognized the good-looking senior fellow walking toward me and waving. His frame was still strong for his apparent age, looking like he had a body for life. He was quick-footed, not remotely like the Mr. Poke-Along I had followed for so long before passing on the road yesterday.

"Hello," I said, reluctant to rush past and be rude. It struck me that his face looked oddly familiar. I couldn't quite place it, and it began the process of nagging me. Was it the beard or the bald crown that was making the connection difficult?

"Good morning. Great spot." He drew to a halt, obviously wanting to have a conversation. He looked at my dripping pant cuffs and smiled. "How much water's in the river?"

"It's high, flowing over 20,000 cfms last week." I decided to answer technically in case he wasn't asking how much water I left in the river after soaking this much up with my pants. "It looks that or more today," I said.

I didn't know if this response would mean anything to him. The San Juan averages less than 1,000 cubic feet per minute of water, so it was really moving.

"That would make a great week down to Cataract Canyon takeout," he replied and flicked at a pesky no-see-um buzzing around us. Amazingly, the blood-sucking little pest left. "Might not even have to paddle."

I chuckled. That told me a lot about him. This much water meant the current was probably running five or six miles per hour, an effortless cruise in a canoe, and he apparently knew it. This also suggested that he knew the flow was probably the same for the Green River, which merged with the Colorado to the north and formed the Cataract Canyon rapids, which was what he was referring to, and that a canoer had better take out of the river ahead of those rapids if he wished to live. The guy had been around this country for sure.

"Yeah," I said, "in fact, the trek would be over too quickly."

It was then that I noticed that under the open collar of his shirt he wore a silver chain. Upon it was an unusual piece of jewelry in the form of delicate silver wings, inlaid with thin splinters of agate and turquoise. It was eye catching, and the strange notion that *he had wings* stuck in my mind. *He had wings*.

I decided to converse with him a little further.

"So, have you seen the pictos?" I asked, referring to the wall of Anasazi pictographs at the back of the camping sites.

By way of an answer, he grinned from behind his groomed silver and gray beard and pulled a small spiral notebook out of his left shirt pocket. He handed it to me. The page it was spun open to had a decent pencil drawing of three anthropomorphs, perhaps from the wall here. I flipped a page or two to see other sketches that recorded these odd triangular human

forms that the ancient Indians drew in special places. I immediately liked the idea of keeping a sketch-pad record. In my
trail-less explorations, I've come across remote art that I was
egotistical enough to believe nobody else had seen. Drawing
them would be much more intimate than a photograph.

"I've seen the wall dozens of times," he added, "and every
time the figures talk to me."

I felt the same way. I handed him back his pad and
whistled in appreciation.

"David," I said, holding out my hand. I don't bother giving
my full name when meeting someone if in all likelihood it will
be just once. Myself, I'm lucky to remember a name after
several meetings. Anyway, who needs last names in the desert?
Keep it simple, I thought.

"We'll both remember that easily enough. Who needs last
names? " He shook my hand firmly. "Keep it simple. I'm also
David."

It threw me off to hear such a resemblance of my thoughts
on his lips. Just a coincidence—but still. He narrowed his
eyes, considering what he had just said, shook his head once,
and then smiled, looking away at the river.

Something about his voice appealed to me. It was cheerful
and uninhibited, but I didn't want to talk right now. I wanted
to change my trousers. Oddly, he just moved off without a
word of leave and walked toward the river.

I was struck again by how strong and limber he looked for
his apparent age. He was about my build and my height, and I

caught myself aspiring to look that good 5, 10, 25 years from now. Except, I thought, Ellen would never go for the facial hair. I tried it once and thought I looked pretty darn good. I believed it somewhat compensated for my slightly severe forehead. Ellen said it made me look villainous and she would definitely not kiss me if I insisted on being scratchy, so I shaved it off. I might try it again someday, though.

I found myself regretting not talking to the gentleman longer as I headed back to camp. I was also thinking, somewhat ashamedly, how I had labeled him while following at his pace on the road yesterday morning.

Lest ye be judged, I reminded myself.

More bad habits to extinguish!

I was in quite good spirits walking back to my tent, even humming a tune. This was yet another demonstration of how effective my survival mechanism had been these six days and nights. Perhaps it just showed the extreme power of what you give your attention to in creating your state of being.

But all the walls were about to come down.

Leaving Your Lane and Crossovers

I'd never seen anything like this rig, and I wanted one. It was evening and I was walking to fill our five-gallon jug at the potable-water spigot near the camp host's site. Ellen and I were tenting this trip, but we also have a high-clearance pop-up we occasionally trailer as well. I tend to think other forms of RV would cramp my style.

This one had my attention. Even the yellow color on the truck works in that particular shade with the smoke-colored camper. The truck had amazing lines, good clearance, yet was extremely low profiled and obviously off-road capable. The camper had electric lifts so it could be left behind in a hurry, in case some adventure beckoned that required the four-wheeling truck alone.

Ellen often talked about other RVs that could meet our needs without being so damn ... whatever! Pick it. She had several complaints. Here, finally, was one that would suit her. She definitely had to see this.

The unique aspect was how the camper worked with the truck. The camper used slider technology in a way I had never seen. It traveled in a short-bed pickup, yet it had two sliding compartments, one pushed out to the left and the other to the right. It must be roomy when expanded.

But the truck displayed something I'm sure didn't come out of Detroit. To accommodate the sliders, the fender walls of the pickup's bed were hinged. They rotated down to the horizontal, extending the bed and supporting the slide-out sections of the camper. Definitely wasn't a Ford. For all that, the camper looked light, and I had already seen that it traveled nimbly and solid without sway. After all, I had followed it yesterday morning for a long time. I'd give anything to see inside that rig.

Just then the owner, David, stepped out of the side door. He had two bottles in his hand. He walked up and popped one into my hand. I said hello again and thanked him for the lager.

"Who makes that?" I pointed the bottle toward his amazing rig as I popped off the cap with my Swiss Army knife. "It's really something."

"Can't get one 'round here, at least not yet," was all David offered. "Want a look?"

"Damn right." I smiled and followed him inside. Normally, I get in trouble for this variety of impulsiveness, disappearing when I was supposed to be gone just long enough for water. Tonight, on this trip, it wouldn't bother Ellen.

I'd never seen anything like the inside of his rig before, and I wanted one for the second time that night. We spent the first beer with my questions about his RV and truck. He was obviously proud of it and loved talking about it.

Normally, I wouldn't have a second drink, but I was enjoying his company, and we were clicking so well that I accepted the offer when it came.

"I'd love to grab Ellen and have her meet you," I said, looking around the inside of his rig again.

He paused for an uncomfortable span of time, and it drew my attention.

"I wish more than anything that was possible." His eyes had become far off, almost sad, but not for himself. It was an extremely odd response, not to mention an alarming contrast to his previous charm. I couldn't explain why, but I didn't want him to clarify that comment. Something in his reaction stirred a thing deep down and dark in me, a thing akin to panic.

To distract myself, I asked where he was traveling.

We were lounging in plush seat-backed cushions that formed three sides of the camper's compact dining table. I was looking at his eyes, familiar in some way, as he explained that he was slowly working his way up to northern Canada, slowly since it was too early to go North just yet.

David paused often while he spoke. His eyes probed me constantly, as if he was working to discover something while we chatted.

We talked for what must have been hours. The man had an amazing calm and poise. He obviously felt good about himself, life, and everything we discussed. His tone was infectious. Also, he clearly had a trust of everything and everyone, stemming not from naiveté but some deeper understanding. As I sat with him, I felt my world expand.

He was going to travel the Alcan Highway on an 8,000-

mile trek. As he described old-growth rain forests, arctic tundra, glacial ice fields, whales and caribou, I was becoming envious. Ever since my brief sojourn to the North, I'd thought about going back to explore it properly. But I'd found neither the freedom nor the time. I still had to work for a living, at least to some extent. I listened intently, though, and, as I did, dared to turn his plans into my own.

At the end of a long tour of the Yukon Territory, he would end up in Vancouver, one of the world's most scenic downtowns, and spend the fall in a skyscraper penthouse facing English Bay, peering up to the Arctic. He'd always wanted to do that. He couldn't say why exactly, except that it was a place that had called to him and he'd discover his purpose there after settling in.

I was so impressed with his manner, his easy freedom to pursue an open-ended life with no worries, that I completely forgot my manners and blurted, "You must have plenty of money stashed away."

He gave me that playful smile. It was long and crafty, surrounded by a strong jaw, stylish moustache, and aristocratic beard. His eyes twinkled with delight as they easily pierced my walls.

"You haven't put it together yet, have you?" he paused. "There is *no such thing* as money."

He sank back into the bench seat.

I was a bit stunned. *Here* was an ancient subject of great power, resistance, and complete distraction. Sure, there was the question of attracting enough, but—no such thing as money? Even if the idea was appealing, it fell short of logic. He might as well be telling me there was no such thing as my electric bill or that, even though I had to purchase gas to get home, my need of cash or a credit card was imaginary. Money in my bank is what had enabled me to buy a house, and to travel here. I told him so.

"The only thing *you* have in your bank is a number that everyone agrees with. You didn't buy your house, or car, with piles of cash; you bought it with a number written on a piece of paper."

I gave a "humph" as I reflected.

"Money is a fiction representing our agreements. That's all. Banks are wonderful institutions that keep the tally; they maintain the balance of agreements made with ourselves, others, and the universe—organized into a convenient number with a dollar sign. It's easily manipulated."

"I've seen plenty of homeless folks that would beg to differ," I noted.

"Some agreements bind us, others free us," he responded.

Then he said, "Work within your agreements, not your dollars. After that you'll never want for money, especially once you've realized that everyone benefits from a good agreement." He grinned.

I raised my beer in salute.

Here was a man to whom our rules didn't apply. But he seemed alone in his journey; and this was an overwhelming topic for me at the moment—unusually so. I couldn't say why.

"I think I would become lonely in your life," I said.

"Now, that would only be possible if I was alone," he rebutted.

He looked alone to me.

"Places aren't the reason to go. Places just create interesting settings," he said.

He leaned forward onto the table. As he did so, the silver talisman shaped like wings and inlaid with agate and turquoise swung forward from the chain around his neck, catching the light. *He had wings.*

"What's your trip about then?" David turned the question on me. "What's the reason behind it?"

I delivered what I thought would be a coy answer with a smile. "This time, I guess, I'm just running away."

My smile wasn't returned, and his eyes became more penetrating. He seemed to find something revealing in that and watched me as if to inquire whether I found anything revealing in that. Finally, he took a sip of his beer.

"Does running away work?" he asked.

"Apparently." I winked at him.

"Apparently." His voice echoed no humor.

The tone of our conversation had suddenly turned some unexpected corner. There was a new look on his face. For the first time, I was uncomfortable in his presence. An awkward silence began and then grew. His eyes bored into me, causing me to start looking away, around, anywhere. Suddenly, I had the oddest feeling of wanting to duck under the table and hide. Finally, when I had become so ill at ease that I was about to break the silence by standing and saying it was late, he spoke, but with a transformed manner.

"That's why I'm here, David, to help." He shifted on the cushion to face me squarely, leaning into the table toward me. "Tell me what's going on."

I was feeling led by the nose. I had some desperate need to explain myself, or at least find a segue into something closer to the previously safe dialogue. To act as if I was complying with his request, I began to speak in generalities about myself, and his mildness returned, which encouraged me.

I hadn't realized how much I needed someone to talk to, and my life started spilling off my tongue. I relaxed a bit and eventually became specific, more personal. Perhaps it should have felt peculiar on a first meeting to open up in this manner. I talked about all the aspects of my life as I now saw them, the changes I was making, how it felt powerful and good, and the earth-shaking events as well. He had genuine interest in every element I shared and constantly asked for details, drawing me further out.

It just followed that I came to describe the recent event that was troubling me, which I couldn't stop thinking about, one for which I still had no answer. Glad of the opportunity to share it, I related my climbing incident.

"I can't get over it," I said. "I never make mistakes like

that. I've cultivated habits to keep me safe in the wilderness. My God, you think you're invulnerable and then an accident like that—"

"So why did you cause it?" he asked.

What?

He had done it again. The awkwardness sprang back into the camper. I'd said *accident*; wasn't he listening?

He waited, watching me.

"I don't know why the damn rock fell!" All of a sudden, I was disproportionately defensive. He was trespassing.

There was that remarkable appeal in his face trying to persuade me, his lips not unpleasant but no smile. He was working my clay like an artisan.

"You do know why," he said as if he had achieved something of the form he wanted.

My head was starting to swim. I had it now; I knew that face. I knew why I had been so comfortable with him straight away. How could I have missed it before?

"No, I really don't know why that damn rock came down!" How could he be here? How could we be talking like this?

"What aren't you telling me, David?" he asked. "What are you leaving out?"

I sat dumbfounded for a long time. I had conveniently forgotten to mention how my own hand pulled out the chock stone and brought the boulder down. I was frozen, confused, and unable to talk.

He looked at me hard and long.

"You were committing suicide."

"What?" I stared horrified into his face.

But it wasn't his face, never had been; it was *my* face, only older. I was unhinging.

He was right. I looked across the table at his lips, my lips, and they spoke the truth. Now that it was voiced, I knew it. I had attempted suicide. My mind stopped working. I couldn't think.

"Why the hell would I do that?" My heart was pounding so loud I could hear it. Time to go, *time to go*!

"The thing is, you didn't, did you? You changed your mind," he said softly.

"That's crazy. Why would I do that?" I felt an instance of vertigo, like falling backward off a ledge I hadn't known was there. The week I had elaborately constructed was disintegrating before me.

"David," he said *our* name, "you know why!"

There were deep pools of compassion in his eyes.

Please don't. Please, no! I can't.

I was on my feet; he was staring up at me from the table.

The avalanche had come.

I ran.

Distant Ambulance

I didn't stop running until I was at our tent. I needed Ellen, desperately. I wanted to hold her, have her hold me. But I was terrified by what I might see when I unzipped the door.

As I looked into the tent, I fell hard to the ground. There weren't two sleeping bags, just mine. Only my pillow, wads of only my clothes. There had never been another occupant in our tent on this trip. My mouth was working silently. My heart was breaking into a million pieces.

I don't know how much later it was that David was there behind me. I was weeping convulsively.

"It was a crossover—" was all I could get out. I didn't turn or look up at him. "She was gone so fast, I never got to say goodbye."

He didn't say a word. Denial was fleeting away as I was finally forced to face my mortal wound, like a stomach-shot soldier, surrendering to the handfuls of spilled gut that he had been trying to scoop back into his belly and, in this last moment, realizing it was over, there was nothing anyone could do. I felt my blood leaving my extremities in a shell-to-core shunt as I started going into shock. I feebly fought it. She had been here, every morning in my arms, sleeping in the Land Cruiser as we drove. At the same time, she couldn't have been. The curtains were stripped away, and her physical absence was laid bare for me to accept.

Ellen had died seven days ago, instantly, in a head-on collision, the very evening we were to depart for the Canyonlands. There had been a tremendous storm. It had occurred on the highway just below our mountain home, so when I got the neighbor's call, I was minutes from the scene, minutes from hopping over the fence at the highway access road and joining the wreckage.

Traffic was built up in both directions under the fog and the gray thunder of rain. Drenched witnesses from the closest cars were out and helplessly scurrying around with no clue of what to do. The sheriff hadn't arrived, due to the clogged traffic arteries. In some hopeless distance, the muted siren of an ambulance, unable to arrive, could be heard.

The driver of the smashed truck was outside in the downpour, either concussive or inebriated, it was hard to tell which. His ruined face had collided with something other than the deployed air bags and was ghoulishly swollen to the size of a pumpkin. He was wobbling from one side of his oversize vehicle to the other, plucking feebly at twisted steel, screaming about some brother trapped inside. The man was oblivious to the bullets of hail pounding him and everything else in the freezing shower. Then, finally, there was what was left of our car, and what was left of Ellen.

I fled the site of the accident in our already prepared and packed Land Cruiser, at high speed, across two states all covered by the same storm. Something or someone had whispered, "Leave!" and I obeyed. My merciful and powerful subconscious found a way to block it all out, purge every shred of the incident in 300 miles of pouring rain.

Now in front of our tent, I was throwing up violently. My gastrointestinal tract was shutting down.

"But she was here!" I choked on my bile. "She was there when the boulder hit me. She was how I got down out of that damn chute. She coached me through every step. I laid in her lap. *She held me!*"

I could still feel her soft thigh, her hand wiping my brow. I knew I hadn't gotten down without her.

I wasn't crazy, was I? I couldn't have invented her being there, too? Emotion exploded from my chest like a cannon.

"*She was here!*" I screamed in utter defiance. ... *Damn it all to hell!*

DAMN.

... damn.

"Yes." David put a strong hand on my left shoulder and squeezed my muscle firmly. "She was here."

His words were liquid confirmation; they held the brilliant white light of truth and comfort. I closed my eyes, sat upright, and wiped bile from my mouth. My emotions went dumb, like the eye of a storm.

She was here. I understood. As sure as my lungs breathed air, as certain as my heart pulsed, she had been here with me, all along, my Ellen. Where was she now?

The older David squeezed my muscle one last time, and then his hand left my shoulder. By the time I managed to turn around to face him, he was gone.

They both were.

I fell apart.

Never Enough Road

There is a bridge between Time and Eternity;
and this bridge is the Spirit of man.
Neither day nor night cross that bridge,
nor old age, nor death nor sorrow.

Upanishads

Fifteen feet on either side of the highway's center line lay a hostile environment. Nine months of the year, it's vicious with heat. The rest of the time, it's just vicious. If any of the occasional travelers, whizzing by in air-conditioned comfort, were to be plucked from the highway's 30-foot delusion and forced into the true nature of this vast Mexican wasteland, they would perish. There's simply no surface water, no escape from the heat and precious little to sustain life.

Creatures that do exist here do so at night and drink the lives of one another. That is the true nature of these badlands, and it has been thus for unmeasured time. Spread out from here, hundreds of miles in all directions, is a forgotten world in which modern man does not belong. Man's a poor observer from a slender asphalt intrusion who flashes past at 100 kilometers an hour. If the highway has shrunk the Sonoran Desert, trivialized or dismissed it, this is so only within the narrow and shoulderless confines of the road.

Unlike other sections of the vast Sonoran, this area is made even more surreal by a moonscape of razor-sharp, iron-colored hills, dense with a needle forest of green saguaro cactus. As far as can be seen, the saguaros form an endless crowd of solitary figures, standing in relentless and unbelievable numbers. Across the flats, through the ravines, up and over the otherwise-naked knife-edge ridges, they stand, stand and wait. They're the land's shaman and the land's knowing, without eyes and blind to their surroundings. They're poised with purpose. Most have arms, many do not, but all of them point the way. And the way is up.

But the solitary man traveling this endless Sonoran road in his dusty blue Land Cruiser had no upward paths. He lived in a two-dimensional world of left and right turns, north and south destinations. And, at the moment, his only concern was to get off the cursed Mexican highway before nightfall. Though the gesturing landscape counseled more, the significance was lost, at least to his conscious mind. It was absurd anyway. There was no way up. His only choice was to go through.

And what he was going through, perhaps the desert alone could abide, this ageless and impassive observer of that which struggles. The Sonoran has ever been an emotionless host that doesn't intervene in the twitching death of a kangaroo rat experiencing the sidewinder's venom, nor judge the end of the snake's starvation. It does not revel in the blossoming of a fragile desert garden or mourn its shriveling in the short life after the rare rainfall that brought it. It neither favors nor hampers but simply allows. This desert, alive with incongruity, was an exquisite equal to the condition of his soul.

In the past, he might have sensed the signs woven in the arid landscape. Not consciously but subtly, experienced as gentle tugs; turn this way, go there, speed up, slow down, like a silent lover pulling on the heart, leading to perfect outcome. He had followed such feelings, impulses we all have but mostly ignore. As a consequence, his life had sprouted magic.

But that was before he was forsaken.

In the past, he had lived for what lay ahead. Now, with singular intention, he was speeding away from what was behind. Having faced the abyss, he'd simply done the only thing he could: he had let go and was in free fall.

• • •

The '70s-vintage Panaderia truck, laboring ahead of me, poured black smoke out of the entire underside of its sizable frame. It was achieving a breakneck speed of 30 kilometers an hour, maybe. It droned obnoxiously. The truck was a damned hazard, since it begged to be passed, but on this narrow, straight Mexican highway, you could only pass blindly. I had a feeling it had been driving in just this condition for 40 years and would still be on this road making deliveries long after I was dead and buried. Its image was doubled in the glistening reflection of a mirage that danced and mirrored a constant distance ahead of me. I stared at the edge of the mirage, watching the lake of water magically evaporate, in perfect jest, before I could reach it. It lulled me.

My head jerked suddenly as the tent trailer bounced badly over another untended section of Mexican highway. As a reflex, I shot a glance at the passenger seat to see if Ellen had wakened. But the seat was littered and empty. Ellen wasn't there. She would never be there again. I stared at the seat she should have occupied.

When I finally looked up, I barely had time to hit the brakes and narrowly avoided smashing into the Panaderia truck, which had come to a full stop in front of me. The tent trailer jackknifed alarmingly into the lane of oncoming traffic before its own surge brakes kicked in and brought it to rest, angled slightly across the highway's center line. The squeal from my brakes and blue smoke from my tires hung in the air.

My sensational stop had caused quite a stir at the front of the short line of vehicles waiting on the highway. Two soldiers bolted into view around the Panaderia truck. They stopped running when they saw that no collision had actually occurred.

As often as I used to vacation in Mexico, I was still slightly unnerved by the automatic rifles so commonly paraded on the shoulders of Mexican soldiers. Coming from the states, I wasn't used to seeing soldiers so prevalently in public, as common as police and with such menacing armaments.

White teeth flashed on the brown faces of the two soldiers as they displayed their amusement at this American's harmless blunder. They walked the rest of the way to my vehicle at a relaxed pace.

"*Pardon, señor, yo quisiera ver su vehículo permitir?*" one of the young soldiers demanded as I lowered the window of my Land Cruiser. I blinked. I had no idea what the man was saying. I wasn't sure I cared. I didn't have the energy to deal with people, much less those I couldn't understand. It made me tired, and my head clouded.

Not for the first time since I left home, I questioned my sanity. I wanted the man to go away, disappear. I wanted to be magically transported to my destination, away from people, away from all civilization, to the secluded ocean cove where the scorching desert sun would burn the grief from my soul. I couldn't endure the time necessary to get me from here to there. It was interminable. Nor could I summon a presence to deal with the authority standing at my truck's window. So I sat dumbly.

The soldier repeated his words, this time with irritation, edging on anger. I just looked at him. I struggled to think of what to do, to communicate somehow. But I couldn't get command of myself, even if it meant offending this Mexican official. I slumped and stared at the empty passenger seat next to me. My heart was gone. The soldier reached out and jerked my door open. I nearly fell out in surprise.

"*Un moment, caballeros de un momento. Soy por favor*

seguro que puedo ayudar en esta materia." A new voice, friendly, mild, coming from down the road, intervened. I looked up from the open cavity of my vehicle at the Mexican civilian hurrying toward the soldier. The man looked like a cowboy, with a large sweat-stained ranch hat shadowing his face. He had big thick hands and a lean strong frame. But he was dressed in relatively expensive attire. He wore crisp new Levi's jeans that accented a shimmering silver Concho belt, polished boots, and a bright plaid long-sleeved shirt. His conversation was a rapid exchange with the soldier, an unintelligible din of Spanish.

Since crossing the border, I hadn't spoken to a soul. I'd hardly spoken to anyone in weeks. I didn't want human contact. I continued listening to the rolling babble of r's and k's, and slipped further into my estrangement.

Therefore, I was shocked when the cowboy Mexican turned and addressed me in English. "*Señor,*" he said, "the officer wishes to know that you are all right but is very upset at your behavior and questions your competence at driving." The streams of words, spoken in English, were like cool water in the desert. I gulped, looking at the Mexican as if he were an angel.

"I'm sorry," I managed. "I was distracted by something in, not in the car, I'm sorry; I didn't see the traffic stopped. I ..."

I shut my mouth. I couldn't stand to listen to myself carrying on like an idiot. I hadn't been myself for quite a while. The cowboy Mexican looked at me for some time, trying to read my face. A shudder built in my chest, something like a

sob but with the momentum of a freight train. I fought to
control it, to keep it down. As I struggled, the Mexican's face
softened. He gave me what felt like a reassuring smile, though
his lips remained pressed and emotionless.

The Mexican returned to his conversation with the soldier,
which lasted quite some time. I watched the arm and hand
gestures of each man, the occasional glance and pointing to
where I sat, and the glares from the soldier. I listened to the
changing tones in their voices. In the end, the soldier folded
his arms smugly across his chest, and the conversation ended.

The cowboy Mexican addressed me again. "I cannot
dissuade the officer from giving you a ticket, and you must
follow him back to Hermosillo to the court there." I clenched.
Three hundred and fifty kilometers back at least, not to
mention the increasing alarm I felt surrounding my growing
predicament. I was being cut from my lifeline, the one thing I
had been able to keep focus on in all these weeks. My ocean
sanctuary was evaporating like the mirage ahead of me.

The soldier spoke again and re-engaged the cowboy. Now
that the engine and air conditioner were shut off, the temperature
on the inside of the Land Cruiser rose steadily. The heat from
the pavement burned into me from the open door. Insects
buzzed around my face, and I began to sweat.

The cowboy Mexican turned back to me when the soldier
finished, this time an unmistakably wide smile unfolding on
his face.

"*Señor*," he said, "the officer, however, has graciously decided that, if you wish, you can pay him for the ticket here. He will spare you the trouble of the drive and his superiors." I began breathing again. I hadn't realized I was holding my breath. It was an obvious bribe, but a break I hadn't expected. My world retreated from the brink as I fumbled for my wallet and asked the cowboy how much.

"No, that will be too much." The man quickly motioned with his hand out of the soldier's sight. "Give him 80." I complied. The soldier then gave me a barrage of Spanish that could have been a lecture or a warning but didn't sound much like a thank-you. The soldier turned his back victoriously and walked to the front of the line of traffic, leaving me with my rescuer.

"Thank you," I said weakly to the man.

"You do not travel lightly, *señor*, that much is clear." The Mexican's ambiguity was skillful and intelligent. "You are vacationing?" he queried.

"No," the word crept slowly from my throat. "Not vacationing, hardly ... escaping, maybe. ... I don't know." I felt oddly at ease with this English-speaking Mexican, a common man, perhaps with some status, judging by the way he was dressed, probably a ranch owner. He possessed a charm.

"I'm going to Playa Cerrar, plan to stay there a while." I curtly offered as a little explanation. I felt indebted to the man. But I really didn't want conversation. Painful memories jabbed at me. La Playa Cerrar. The secluded cove that Ellen and I frequented through our college years, our own personal desert oasis. Only local Mexicans went to that rugged area. Few Americans knew of it. A friend of ours had discovered it by boat years ago and reported there was something of a road leading to it from the scorched hills.

We had made quite a project of finding the route in. We spent three trips and countless hours. It had been more than we hoped for, a gem in our life. But that had been a long time ago, before new cars, houses, kids, and careers. I didn't know what to expect now. I was drawn there against all reason. At the same time, I dreaded returning and dwelling among the ghosts of my past.

"I know it well, Playa Cerrar," the Mexican said to my surprise. "I have spent much time there myself. Usually in the winter, *que no*, when it is bearable." The cowboy's eyes sparkled a little as he poked fun at me, seeing how this was the height of summer. We looked at each other, and the conversation stalled.

A loud honk from the army jeep on the side of the highway pierced the air. All the other vehicles, aside from the Mexican cowboy's late-model quad-cab Ford and my rig, had been waved on. The soldiers were gesturing to me and the Mexican. The cowboy shrugged, grinned, and said no more. I watched as he walked to his truck, got in, and drove the short distance to the jeep. Another short conversation occurred up there, and then the cowboy and his truck departed. To my amazement, the two soldiers climbed into their jeep, kicked up a cloud of dust as they spun off the sand, and also disappeared down the highway.

As abruptly as my solitude had been shattered, it was re-stored. I sat numbly listening to the sweltering desert sounds; an occasional furnace wind kicked up from uneven heating, a steady ticking from some unimaginable insect. The mirage still danced ahead of me, on the highway and out into the Sonoran Desert. I watched.

My love was there, though I couldn't know it. She was in the desert, in the landscape. The solitary Sonoran knew of her and spoke for her. She whispered through its desert wind. But the stirrings were unable to penetrate the mirage sweltering in front of my eyes. Even so, she knew the appropriateness of my struggle and waited with infinite patience.

Cross, Head, and Tail Winds

The sky was wrong. The sudden drop in temperature was welcome, but the raw power in the atmosphere should have been disturbing, would have been disturbing had I been looking at it. Its composition was ill-made; the thin fabric of the desert sky, normally brilliantly clear and kissing with heat, was being brutalized with an overwhelming burden. It simply wasn't going to support the weight of the moisture streaming in long black tendrils from the Baja's gulf.

The darkness above was three-dimensional, reaching high with icy malice and tumbling cascades of black water vapor, extending wide in a horrific march that was rapidly slaughtering the arid blue remnants of the afternoon. On the earth, the desert was on edge, for it was incapable of withstanding the inevitable assault. The ground here had been sculpted by eons of heat to the purposes of baking, like clay oven bricks. It didn't have the capacity to absorb the quantities of moisture that were assuredly coming. The desert's stronghold in the air above was going to fall, and there would be no ground defense.

Yet thus far, the darkening land remained dry, and there wasn't even a breath of a breeze.

And there wasn't a breath of oxygen left in my lungs. Even though my chest squeezed with pain and my gut panicked from lack of oxygen, I remained submerged in the violent water, resisting the cries of need from my body. I pushed my toes deeper into the slimy moss covering the bottom of the rock floor, trying to reinforce my purchase and withstand for a little longer the force of the torrent working to sling me backward.

My body wrenched and jerked in the stream jettisoned from the inverted geyser, shooting into the cistern from above. The water was geothermal and came from a mammoth rusted pipe whose ejecting end was suspended a few feet up from the rock walled pool. The outpour scrubbed every nerve on the surface of my body raw, and the full force of it seemed to be blasting a hole through my chest. It palpitated my cheeks, crushed my closed eyes, wiped my mind, and cleansed my very soul.

But this purging wasn't why I remained submerged. Rather, it was because there, in the cacophony of water, whether real or imagined, was Ellen. I had a sense of her, folded in the torrent. I could almost hear her in the muted roar. Somewhere just out of reach, she embraced me between heartbeats.

Each time the urgency screamed from my lungs and my torso clamped with nausea from asphyxiation, I refocused on the stream. I reached deep into the current, and my physical washed away. I managed to remain submerged, seconds passing like centuries, until my body would stand for it no more. I had pushed too far. My mouth was going to open; my lungs were going to fill themselves at any second, with either water or atmosphere. It wouldn't matter. I had to choose.

I chose air, life.

I leaped up and out of the 5-foot-deep pool into the full force of the water bulleting from the irrigation pipe. The hydrant's blast slammed me backward, causing me to travel the 12-foot length of the cistern in a flash, threatening to break my head on the stone and mortar walls that damned the water aft.

I let the force of the current suspend me against the back wall while I recovered my breath. My lungs gulped air in powerful heaves. The water surged around my shoulders trying to regain the outlet I was blocking. When I recovered sufficiently, I fought my way forward once again into the geyser and dived just under the pipe where the current was the strongest. I repeated this submerged communion again and again, the storm forming in the sky above be damned.

Eventually, I moved sideways out of the flow, exhausted, and perched my armpits on the thick stone walls of the irrigation cistern. Resting my chin on my forearms, I looked out across endless acres of fine clay soil crowded with dehydrated cotton plants. The cotton balls were fat and ready for plucking. Escaped cotton fibers were entangled on scratchy brown leaves, and countless white strands were tethered along the mosaic floor of cracked clay. My body floated seductively, since the current was somewhat gentler here on the side. All around me the air was filled with a constant roar from the pipe's shooting water.

As I floated in the warm water, the hole opened up in me again. I was never going to get over this. She couldn't be gone. Hadn't I just spoken to her? She had wanted me to water the tomato, green chili, and jalapeño salsa garden. Weren't we going to rebuild the deck this fall?

The Mexican terrain was swept away, replaced by the last images I had of our house. Her things had still occupied every room. The clothes her warm body had filled lay on chairs. Her makeup bottles were strewn atop the cabinet above untidy drawers. She was always running late; that's why the bedroom was a jumble. Ellen usually picked up her clutter when she got home. But she'd never return from her last errand. Evidence of her life was everywhere, in every room. And on our bed, in the covers, on the pillow, her scent lingered.

I wasn't able to lie in that empty bed. After finding my way home from Utah, I attempted sleeping in the master bedroom's sitting chair instead. That was perhaps worse. From the chair's vantage, moonlight bled through a high clerestory window, bathing the bedroom in gray silhouettes; and the scene tortured me until twilight.

I lasted exactly two nights.

"I'll be all right." That's what I had told David Jr. at the airport. A piece of him had died, too; even across state lines, he and Mom had never gone more than a few days without talking. Amber was returning to her first year of college. I could feel the hurt she buried in impenetrable silence as she hugged her goodbyes. She worried me, but probably not as much as I worried her. I had frightened her by vanishing from the scene of Mom's accident, scared them both. But they accepted my assurances that I'd faced what I needed out there in the canyons. They would've never left me standing there in that airport had they known the whole canyonland story.

I'd told them both I could cope, but by the second night, alone in my bedroom, it was clear—I couldn't. Around one a.m., I dug myself out of the master bedroom's sitting chair and drove under headlights, down the black and empty rural road, to my office. There, on the reception area's sofa, I collapsed into a coma of sleep.

"Out of the office—return uncertain." That was the automated response I tapped out on my office keyboard the next morning. This robotic reply to e-mails and sales queries would slowly murder the prospering company I'd built. I suppose I knew that. But it was the only message I could manage.

Then I picked up the office handset and called David and Amber to say I couldn't face the mountain home. To soften it, I added, "Just not yet." Still, that felt like deception. No matter how I dressed it up, I was running away.

My kids needed me, and they needed me to be well. I told them I would be, but they'd have to trust me to find my way. It was asking a lot after the scare I gave them. In the end, what choice did they have? I left.

"Oh God, Ellen," I cried beneath the thundering irrigation pipe, "God ... God damn."

Through tear-filled eyes I watched the water stream out of my mossy bath, down chipped and broken-brick-lined channels that conveyed their water to the parched fields. The flowing sight slowly coaxed me from this episode of grief, and I became numb once more. I stowed my heart again for the millionth time.

These fields will always be thirsty, I thought glibly, given just enough to struggle, stuck neatly between life and death.

The Mexican agricultural project, built by German engineers, was a questionable ploy to farm the desert. It was leaching the life out of the poor desert soil. While the crop undeniably grew, it looked propped up and scared. Even though man had found a wealth of water deep under the ground, the natural desert seemed offended by this indecorous sin.

On the other hand, the rock-walled irrigation cisterns placed strategically through the giant project formed an oasis for the local workers, and for me. Their value was immeasurable.

As I floated, attached to the wall and lost in myself, the first salvo of rain hit. I barely noticed it, since the air around me was singing with mist and droplets from the irrigation pipe. However, the astonishing difference in raindrop temperature soon got my attention. The drops from the sky were like needles of ice stinging my arms, a cutting contrast to the hot springs in which I bathed.

I looked up, taking note of the foreboding sky. By now it was completely black, and the early afternoon had prematurely darkened. I noted that it was going to storm and let it go at that. I was remotely curious about what that would be like in this desert; I had never experienced rain here. It was an underreaction to the severity of the conditions, but I wasn't to blame. After all, I had little experience with the weather possibilities on this Mexican coast. And even among locals, only the oldest would be able to recall anything like what was approaching.

I elected to watch the rain from the cistern. For the first time since I had arrived at this incinerated coast, I was actually physically comfortable. The chill air was wonderful. The water heated from deep in the bowels of the Earth felt incredibly nurturing. I watched as the rain came down, beating the ground, causing little explosions of dust with each raindrop's strike. Then I watched as the ground formed a film of mud where the water accumulated. In only a matter of minutes, the ground was saturated. Pools formed and combined, then swelled. Streams began to flow in all directions.

Now I re-confirmed my decision to stay in the cistern— for warmth. It was becoming downright inhospitable out there. I was thinking I'd delay until this desert thunderstorm passed. So I waited. Streams were now combining to form small rivers on the dirt road and around the rock and mortar walls where I bathed. I watched the muddy rivulets as they began churning with miniature rapids. It soon became apparent that I might not be able to wait this squall out after all.

With utter disgust, I pulled myself out of the seductive warm water and climbed onto the slippery ledge of the cistern. There I stood, five feet in the air, stark naked in the icy rain.

"Well," I muttered, "this is inconvenient."

After a moment of arctic abuse, I bolted toward the Land Cruiser, which was parked next to the main irrigation ditch, splashed through mud, and climbed in, sticky, wet, and cold. I groaned when I realized I had sat on, and completely soaked, my clothes that were strewn across the front seat. After toweling myself off as best I could in the cramped confines of the vehicle, I put on the clothes and endured their grimy wet patches that clung uncomfortably to my skin.

I fired up the engine to get the heater going and remained parked. By now the water was flowing down the front windshield in cascades. I shivered and turned on the wipers full speed. That helped somewhat. At least I could see the dirt road intermittently. It was running with water.

Time stood still as the wipers swept buckets of water off the windshield. Pain and loss built until I wept. "Ellen, I can't go on." My tears spent themselves, only to build again as I sat there, a puppet in the storm. Between the waves of emotion, I was just worn out and sad. In those emptied moments, I once again had a notion of Ellen there. I could find her; she was just there on the edge, in the fringe of light, waiting for the waves of grief to subside. I felt I should try to reach out, but it was just too much. I couldn't, not now.

Out of nowhere, a small green Datsun with Arizona plates

gingerly picked its way past my parked Land Cruiser. Gad! I didn't know Datsuns still existed. Ellen and I used to have one. It was soon out of sight, swallowed by the sheets of rain. I remained parked a while longer but eventually eased my truck onto the road. For good measure, I reached down and locked the transfer case into four-wheel drive as I drove. I made a series of turns through the acres of industrialized farm and was soon on the rugged road that led to the ocean.

The Datsun, though well ahead of me, was also on this remote road. I could see its brake lights occasionally up ahead.

The rain let up, easing to a thin periodic weep. The sky looked no better. As I traveled, the land changed from the flat tabletop desert; it fell away in front of me and the Land Cruiser entered the mouth of a long narrow canyon that spectacularly carved its way down several hundred feet to the ocean.

I slowly picked my way down tight twists in a terrain lined with organ-pipe cactus and walled with chipped and eroded rock giving way to sloping hills, an ancient wash filled with sand in some places and broken volcanic basalt in others. The sandy bed that was here had done a better job of absorbing the rain than the clay desert above. No water flowed.

The descent eased, the road leveled, and the cactus and elephant trees on either side became strewn with trash. Everything from cartons and bottles to sun-bleached rags littered the ground. Papers and plastic bags blown here from decades' worth of Mexicans on holiday decorated the limbs of spiny bushes. Finally, the road broke out to the pebble beach of an isolated circular cove. Cliffs marched down from high on either side of the cove and dived into the waters. The wide lagoon was breathtaking. A bullet-shaped island of rock with spines of saguaro cactus stood a couple of miles out, picturesquely framed in the center of the small bay.

The ocean that normally swept the beach in gentle waves was now furious with white caps. The cannon thunder from the tumbling surf was clearly audible even through the closed windows of the Land Cruiser. My tent trailer stood on the high ground of the beach. On the low ground, near the water's edge, was parked the green Datsun.

I was pretty sure that if I ignored it, the Datsun should disappear. "For Christsake, leave me alone," I muttered inhospitably.

I parked next to my trailer. The heater in the truck had warmed me through. As I opened the door to get out I noticed the air had recovered some of its desert warmth since the rain had paused.

I walked through crunchy gravel and sand to the tent trailer door, opened it, and stepped in. Next came the task of unzipping the canvas curtains that covered the plastic windows so I could watch the scene from within. This morning's coffee still sat on the propane stove. I lit a burner and set the pot on it to reheat, then peeled off my wet clothes. By the time I'd toweled myself and put on dry garments, my coffee was boiling ruinously. I sniffed the brew, poured a cup, and sat on the cushioned bench seats. With cup in hand, I propped my elbows on the RV's small yellow table that attached to the wall under the sleeping compartment and let the steam from the mug rise to my face.

My attention was drawn outside as the door of the Datsun popped open. Out jumped two occupants. Though they were a distance away, I could easily make out their features. The boy was clean cut, wore a billowy long-sleeved cotton shirt and half-legged flopping short pants. He walked with his hands in his pockets, kicking shells and rocks along the gray beach.

The girl was outrageous. Oblivious to the threatening black sky and white caps, she wore a minimal green bikini. She charged straight into the ocean and jumped and danced with her arms in it. She splashed water playfully at her companion, turned, and swirled.

I couldn't help but smile as I watched their abandon; two college kids, sneaking down here for a break, short of time and living fully for every second.

But this scene was too familiar, bringing out poignant memories of my own past in this cove. I decided to believe that these new neighbors out there on the beach were not real. I attributed what I was seeing to grieving, like watching an old movie. Perhaps their invasion of my solitude made sense in some dysfunctional way. From the point of view of my ramshackle life, these two were here to torment me.

Ah, my limb. It's gone. I could still feel it moving. Surely, I would look and there it would be. ... No, just this terrible hole where a part of me had been.

I missed her. What could I do?

Without warning, the rain started again. The two kids darted for their car like beach crabs scurrying for cover. It wasn't long before they reemerged, more appropriately dressed. They opened the trunk, gathered armfuls of camping gear, and ran for the cliff wall at the far edge of the cove. As I watched, they set up camp under the slight overhang of rock, which was affording some shelter from the rain. I had an impulse to go out there. I decided not to. They might melt away, as does a mirage. So instead, I sat in my trailer, remaining the isolated observer.

Traveler in the Storm

The afternoon turned to evening, and now the cove was besieged by the storm. The rain was strong, cold, and it poured solidly without stop. A barrage of water pellets hit the fiberglass roof and noisily filled the tent trailer with a crackling and unnerving sound. Low-pitched booms from the crashing surf underscored the din.

I was trying to read a science-fiction novel to bide the time but couldn't get my heart in it. Time crept by painfully, slowly, and I fidgeted between reading, watching the waves in the dimming light, and listening to the harangue of the storm.

Finally, it became dark enough that I thought I could make an attempt at bed. I climbed into the canvas-lined compartment above the table and squirmed into my sleeping bag. Amazingly, I actually fell asleep.

My dreams were macabre, horribly real, not like dreams at all.

I die. In fitful dreams, over and over, I die with her, on the road to our mountain home, on that any ordinary day. It's raining, cold, and then from nowhere a truck flashes between strokes of the wiper blades, head-on into our windshield. Such energy, such speed, her eyes are fixed, a colliding force of over a hundred miles an hour. Flying knives of steel, plastic and glass halt in midair to become a jagged wall, and she goes through it. Some pieces of shrapnel pierce her heart, pierce my heart. Others rip open her throat, our throats. I slump with her, watching life's final events through curtains of rain. Her eyes soften, my eyes soften. Our heart stops beating.

All night long, I departed with her as that dream replayed. I couldn't get her attention, could only watch and call her name. "Ellen, what are you doing? Why are you doing this?" I tossed in my sleeping bag, twisted and turned as I rode in a bright tunnel with her. Down the corridors of white with breathtaking speed, her hair blowing, but oddly her focus was on me. Her face was calm, at peace with a certainty and purpose. Bliss graced her cheeks. She couldn't see me; I wasn't really there. Limp and lifeless arms couldn't reach for me. Down the highway, again and again, the half-dream replayed faster and faster, blinding, dizzying,

I sprang awake as the canvas from above the sleeping compartment slammed down on my head. The canvas retreated and surrealistically rose like a balloon inflating, then once again careened downward as another gale force blasted. The metal frame that supported the canvas and the tent trailer was groaning, screeching in agony. The wind came in powerful gusts, and with each gust I could feel the interior walls of the trailer bend and distort alarmingly. Between blasts the trailer worked to regain its boxy shape.

As I lay there, the storm rocked me spasmodically. I recounted the strange dream there in the darkness until I couldn't anymore. I knew. It didn't help my pain, but now I knew. "Oh, Ellen, it *was* your time, wasn't it?" From my dark and tortured sleeping chamber, to the wind I said, "Fly her home."

This was her storm, her triumph.

I zipped the sleeping bag down to vent some heat and flopped my arm out. It must have been raining sideways with the wind because I could feel the seams where canvas connected to the metal flowing with water. In the near blackness, I listened to the storm and tried to accept it. I resisted the fear that the canvas top of the tent trailer might be ripped away and take off like a kite. Instead, I forced myself to appreciate that it was intact, appreciate my shelter. The storm wouldn't invade this cocoon. That was something I inexplicably knew.

There was no letup. I lay there for what seemed an eternity, listening to every sound of complaint from the trailer, estimating its strength during each assault and feeling its recoveries. There was no end to the night.

Finally, I got up and lighted the electric lamp above the galley. The scene was even more disturbing in the yellow light. The whole frame kept bending away from the ocean, and then it would right itself. Some gusts actually lifted the trailer slightly. The pounding from the rain and roar from the ocean were constant. The trailer was obviously going to need repair. But I was confident it would stay together.

Anyway, I detected that the force of the storm was beginning to decrease, if ever so slowly. I decided to cook a meal. Reaching into the small refrigerator, down and to the left of the stove, I rifled for foodstuff and then stood with a carton of eggs.

As I reached for a frying pan, from the corner of my eye, I noticed Ellen behind me, sitting at the camper table in her familiar body; a mental aberration. It was a melancholy wisp of imagination, just a detour in a stream of thoughts, all conceived and forgotten in less than a breath. I plopped a lavish amount of butter into the pan and lighted the burner.

I was emotionally spent. The dream, the storm, and the full realization of her end had left me utterly numb. It was a merciful release, to feel nothing; for the first time in an eternity—*to feel nothing*. No pain, no squeeze on the heart, no hopeless grief. Nothing! I was simply going through the motions of life, heart pumping blood, lungs breathing air, mind empty, mercifully numb.

This empty space opened the tiniest crack for which something outside had patiently waited. For the briefest of moments, my heart was a blank page that could be written upon. But that moment was enough.

The butter sizzled, emitting an aromatic steam that filled my nostrils.

It came through the source—feelings.

I feel powerful. God, I feel powerful. I reached and opened the egg carton and swirled back to the fry pan.

I am happy, uncommon, powerful, happy. Looking up from the stove, the inside of the camper looked cheery to me, very cheery indeed.

There is no pain, only joy, whispered around me, through me. I started to dance, actually danced in front of the stove, swaying my hips. I found myself humming as I cooked. *La, tah dah*—dance, chuckle, grin, dance, and on ...

. . . and ...

I suddenly stopped.

As quickly as it had appeared, that bizarre jubilation vanished. The familiar hollowness resumed. I froze, dead on my feet. It was like noticing a wind, only because it had stopped blowing. My hands hung above the stove.

"For heaven's sake, isn't the feeling of abandoned joy just a tad out of place for me about now?" I screamed to my vacant surroundings.

—glad you noticed.

My head jerked upright. I suddenly felt quite dizzy. I whispered the question, "Who's there?"

The answer ejected me from my natural body. ... "Ellen?"

Ellen!

"Oh my!"

Two eggs sizzling in butter as I stood above the stove, rocking with the trailer and smelling the aroma—these were the last physical sensations I remembered. Then I was above, around, nowhere, everywhere—suddenly looking down at myself. And it was so far down, down there to where my tiny body stood, leaning motionless over the distant yellow stove in the far-off canvas trailer.

Seconds, minutes, hours, days—I didn't know. Time ceased to be, and I soared. I was gone from the world.

Without a doubt it was Ellen. I shared in the experience of what it was where she was. All the things that were held as separate in my world combined to become one as I departed above myself in hers. Nothing was material. Matter had merged with non-matter, canceling exactly. The illusion of *having* and the anguish of *wanting* extinguished each other. Pleasure joined with hurt. Fulfillment and longing linked and ceased to be. Despair and hope. All opposites merged, recombined and annihilated to the state of origin, until all that remained was one singular thing—joy, all that ever was; in the beginning, and in the end.

There was no pain.

There is no pain, only joy.

New Road

Utter Despair must surrender all love
As absolute love does surrender all despair

(transliterated on the dawn of day one)

It took a while for me to slip back into my body. Was that my voice chuckling?

"How incredible!"
"How familiar!"

I had no grief. Like turning off a switch, it was just gone. Impossible! It should take a lifetime to end such grief, if ever it would end. No one will believe this. A door had opened that wouldn't close again.

Vanquished!

In time to come, I would see that Ellen, from the eternal, had bestowed an uncommon gift last night. But at the moment, I wasn't thinking a thing. I was basking.

I sat on the tent trailer's cushioned bench in yellow warmth as the gray dawn woke the shore. Pelicans screeched and swooped in the shallow lagoon. There was not even a breath of a breeze, and the rain was gone. The wondrous beat and rhythm of the crashing waves filled the trailer. Crisp, clean sea air filled my nostrils. The atmosphere was alive.

Slowly it occurred to me that there was something else in the sound-scape. There was a pounding, but not of nature, steady, louder.

Someone was knocking at the trailer door.

I slid out from under the table, walked to the center of the camper, reached and turned the handle. The door swung open. There stood the handsome college lad in the morning light.

I should have been shocked, for I actually recognized this young man, though he couldn't possibly know me. I had also recognized his companion, and, of course, all this was implausible. But surprise wasn't on the radar, not after what had been imparted to me in the dark and early morn. Instead, it was amazement. It was magic. It was anticipation. With last night, I thought it was ended. Ellen's voice answered for the very last time,

—No ... it is begun.

• • •

When I watched them yesterday, I had believed those two kids were ghosts, shadows formed in my mind. Now here the lad stood, as if materialized into my world.

I was just going to have to go with this one, see where it led.

I considered the fellow at my door.

He looked distraught, and that struck me as odd. There couldn't possibly be a thing in this glorious world to make him look like that.

"Good morning," I said cheerfully. His face was dreadful.

"Please, I need your help," he said quickly. He looked over his shoulder,

"It's filling up. She ... Ah shit, just come on."

"What's wrong?" I said as I jumped down onto the ground from the camper.

Even though I should have been prepared, the sight was a shock, and I froze in midstep. On the far side of the cove, against the cliff wall, was the kid's camp. It looked to have weathered fairly well, considering. The tan tent was collapsed in just one place where a tent pole had given way. Consequently, the rain fly was dimpled and held a pool of water visible even from across the cove. Everywhere, things were soaked. But as I stood on the rise where the tent trailer and truck were parked, it was the sight between me and their camp that wasn't credible.

There was a river, deep and narrow, where none had existed before. It was rushing through the center of the beach, if you could still call it a beach. The pebble sand was basically gone, washed to sea. The water-swollen canyon above had created a flood that carved a 6-foot-deep ravine between the two cliff sides of the cove. Through this new gorge, angry water raged.

And in the middle of that river, at the lowest point and alarmingly close to the ocean, was the green Datsun. It was submerged to the door handles, with water pounding along both of its sides and over the hood. I ran with the boy to the edge of the flash flood.

From the steamed window of the passenger-side door, I could make out the shape of a trapped and panicked face peering out.

Road Service

There is only perfection,
And a tremendous rarity of those who observe it,
(transliterated on the morning of day one)

The morning in the desert coastal cove opened like an oyster. The dome-topped island, a few miles from land, wore a crown of billowing clouds, and beyond the island the canvas of ocean and sky was streaked with orange, pink, and blue. The dawn lighted the world and presented the pearl that the storm had created: water in the desert.

A cool, misty fog, waist high, treated the floor of the sloping hills that led to the canyon's rim. Small animals, usually nocturnal, were out in the gray morning light, darting with delight between the cactus and bushes as they sipped the droplets that decorated the plants. The rarified gift of abundant moisture was causing tremendous celebration.

However, from the perspective of so many human recipients, the morning was a wreck. That certainly was the dominant experience of those in the desert flatlands above the canyon as they dealt with cataclysmic damage. As for here, in the canyon below, it was utter panic for two of the three witnessing the earth-changed cove at la Playa del Cerrar.

For the third—me—standing on the newly cut bank of the newly born river, it was nothing short of dazzling.

The college boy was frightened to his core and frantic with the need for action. But what action, what to do?

It was making him desperate. His car below was being swallowed by the torrent of water. The only possible escape was through electric windows, and the car battery was under water, shorted out and useless. His companion was going to be swept out and drowned by the sea, entombed in a two-door green metal coffin made in Japan. She was crying with her hands on the glass. There was no reasonable way down the 6-foot sheer wall of sand that was still breaking off and falling into the rushing water. He was close to taking the unreasonable way down as he paced back and forth, estimating the speed and raw force of the floodwaters.

However, in the afterglow of last night's bequest, it was difficult for me to believe in crisis. I should have suppressed myself. I should have at least summoned enough delicacy to realize how chuckling might affect this urgent young man prancing at my side. But I was still connected to whatever experience I had last night, one foot here, the other a step over the threshold. And I knew, from sand, water, and sky, that Ellen's storm had no harm in it for this couple. I knew from the future. I knew from the past. I knew from the present, where time does not exist. I saw only perfection this morning; the dawn after the victory of my lover's rain. There was nothing else, and I was electric with feelings, not the least of which was good humor. With some detachment, I observed the un-folding events and realized they lacked nothing. For an instant, I clearly saw my place in them.

The clarity was delicious.

As for the other two, well, they were like frightened puppies strongly in need of reassurance.

I looked away from the green submarine and was startled by the dead anger growing on the face of the college lad. I immediately realized my blunder. I toned my mood down a few notches, lest I become the target of the boy's need for action. I reached out to put a reassuring arm on the boy. The kid whipped his shoulder away like a street fighter and lifted his hands. Weight-trained biceps bulged and stretched his short sleeves.

"Are you nuts?" the boy screamed and cried.

I backed up and gestured with palms down in what I hoped looked like the universal signal of *just hold on a minute.* My demeanor was enough out of place in this crisis that it gave me a certain advantage. Perhaps there was something in my body language that was calming. The girl in the car down below was peering up. Her chest and face occasionally shook with convulsive gasps. She was no longer sobbing.

"Whoa," I said, "hang on there. She's going to be all right." I turned to the car and formed a circle with my left thumb and index finger and slowly mouthed *okay* to the girl.

"Look." I turned back to the college kid. "This isn't a real river, you know that; it's temporary, made by the storm. And see, it isn't rising anymore. It's falling." I pointed out that the water that had recently been pouring steadily over the car hood now was just occasionally brushing its top. The boy followed.

The red-cheeked mute watched from behind glass in her isolation chamber at what appeared to be thoughtful explanation and planning occurring up on the bank. This denoted rescue to her, and she eased a little more.

"And the tide"— this time the kid offered no resistance when I took his shoulder and gently turned him to the cliff walls while I pointed—"is going out, not coming in. I've been here for weeks. I know the patterns. Trust me, high tide is just about now."

The surf was fully engaged in the cove, and there were no signs of low water, such as exposed rock with barnacles on the cliff walls to either side.

"She's going to be fine," I said. "All we need to do is wait a spell. I don't see any water to speak of in there with her, do you? The worst thing we can do is break her window and try to pull her out through that current."

I paused and looked at the young man, letting him absorb it. The boy's handsome face was struggling. It was obviously difficult for him to make the transition, to quell the adrenaline rush of urgency and accept that the best course of action might be no action.

"Your car can be dried out in a hurry, you know," I added. "This is the desert."

I waited some more, then said, "Come on, sit."

I slowly sat a few feet back from the edge of the ravine while still holding on to the arm of the kid. He followed me dumbly to the ground and looked back and forth from the hood of the car to where the remnants of the beach met the ocean. I repeated calming gestures to the girl in the half-buried Datsun. The boy was beginning to believe it—he, too, signaled to her, trying to convey with hand signals the way things were improving.

That did the trick. She craned her neck, turning her head as she surveyed her situation as if for the first time. She looked at the hood of her car and then stretched tall to see the outside door handle. She was catching on. Amazingly, she nodded with comprehension, signaling back *okay*. I allowed the smile to return to my face.

So there we sat, all three watching the water, each other, waiting, not communicating as the river pounded the car and the ever-present surf of the ocean tumbled and crashed to the shore. I breathed the salt air being warmed by the rising sun.

Still immersed in the afterglow of last night's communion, all the morning's colors were more vibrant and the sounds distinct. My head was clear; it was like experiencing, for the very first time, the life I had known before life. It was an unimportant mistake that I assumed this incredible sensation would endure.

I watched the girl with her head on the seat rest, eyes locked on the boy above as the morning sang patiently along.

Ellen had a way with her eyes like that; it had been an endearing quality I always loved.

I was the first to break the silence.

"Um ... what's she *doing* in the car?" I asked with just a hint of renewed humor. "I mean, forgive the obvious question, but I'm dying to know. You're out here, she's in there?"

The boy's mood was thick and he clouded over. "Storm was bad in a tent," he muttered. "The tent was actually pretty wild a few times, laying down on us in the wind and all." He looked at me. "It's a good tent, alpine mountaineering tent, bivouac, built for it. I spent over 400 bucks on it." The boy looked out toward his camp and at the marvelous geodesic-framed nylon shelter. "It can take it."

"Yeah, good tent," I echoed.

"She didn't think so. And our sleeping bags had gotten a little wet before I had the tent flap secured. She wanted to move to the car."

He smiled down at her just in case she might be capable of reading lips and then looked at me again.

"I didn't want to get drenched leaving the tent. I can't sleep in that cramped little car. I knew we'd sleep better in the tent even with the noise. Look at it, two seats and a steering wheel. Nobody could sleep in that!"

"Good point." I kept a poker face.

After a summary pause, I asked innocently, "Get any sleep?"

The boy shot a look at me, and a flash of anger transformed to something else in his eyes. Then he mooed like a cow, "No."

The kid huffed out a half-laugh, and I completely cracked up. He lifted his head, smiling with embarrassment. Then we both laughed. The girl looked at us incredulously through the glass.

"She's going to be mad at you, you know," I said finally.

"I don't think she'll be thinking about that." The boy turned to the car and gestured a hug to his girl. She melted and gestured back, with a kiss.

"Oh no, she won't be mad, not now, uh-uh. Just for the next 25 years, every time she retells the story to you or your friends," I said with some authority on the subject.

The boy pressed his lips hard around a smile and peered deeply into the car. "We're not *married*." He grinned.

No, not yet, I thought. I looked back and forth between the two of them and enjoyed the private thread of familiarity I was sharing with them.

The boy grabbed and shook my hand with strength and sincerity. He paused and looked at me. "Thank you." He lit up.

I watched the car, watched the water. Time passed as dawn moved to early morning and then some. Desert heat immediately flamed into the cove as the sun peaked over the canyon ridge behind us. Though the climate quickly transformed, there was coolness remaining in the sand from last night's deluge. This allowed us to continue to sit with some comfort. Eventually, it became obvious to both of us that it was time for the rescue.

Without even a glance at each other, we both stood. I walked to the Land Cruiser. It was a serious off-road vehicle, and Ellen and I had always kept gear in the back for off-road mishaps. Soon I returned with a shovel and a bucket. The water was slowing to a slumbering flow. The two of us scrambled down the crumbling bank and set to the task of digging and clearing the passenger car door in the gathering heat.

An hour later, with us drenched in sweat, enough of the wet sand had been removed to free the door slightly. It screeched open 6 inches. I squatted. Putting my hands on my knees, I said, "Pleased to make your acquaintance."

Her face brightened. She opened her mouth, dropped her tongue, and mocked panting.

She was lovely. Even after that strenuous night and panicked morning, she remained striking. Her hair, the color of sunset, was cut short to the collar. She had an absolutely perfect nose above subtle lips and delicate chin. Observing her youth, I was filled with the desire to shield this sweet lady, decades younger than me, protect her from what was to come. At the same time, I knew that such was not within my power. This thought was a deep sadness.

I blinked as I noticed something in my borrowed bliss take a step back from me. In its retreat, I felt I had suddenly diminished. The habit of life was slipping thickly back onto my shoulders. But it wasn't as heavy to wear at the moment; for now I knew what it felt to be unencumbered. I wanted to restore that feeling of utter liberation. However, it wasn't mine, and I would have to win it for myself. Last night's grace was but a sign pointing the way, the one at last I should follow.

I deliberately focused on gentler tones; the sound of the surf and the call of seagulls, the relief surging in my companions, and the thrill of the adventures assembling and starting to unfold.

"Get me the hell out of here," was what she said next.

"You heard the lady." I grinned. With several grunts, we pried open the door, a bit farther, against wet sand.

I reached down to help her up. When her hand took mine, that's when I sensed him through the soft touch of her skin. I could actually feel him there. Without words, he spoke.

He was asking me to save him.

I was startled. I'd never been told, never once consulted— I had never known he needed saving.

Places

I was born with the notion of the great things I should do.
But achieving them proved impossible.
Yet greatness abounds in every millimeter of wonder
between me and an adorned alpine lake. From the majestic
snow-corniced summit and head wall that provide the crys-
tal water to the white heather at my feet and every insect,
cool breeze in the fir, and bold jay between. It is everywhere
outside of me, and never was inside of me.
So it is true that greatness is actually easy, for all I
need do is join with that that already is. And let it work as I
incorporate with it.
Then stay silent about it. For recognition from others
threatens destruction of my ability to achieve it further.

(transliterated on the afternoon of day one)

It didn't hurt—amazingly, there was no pain at all as I watched those two hold each other in the new arroyo of the ruined beach. I could feel the place where my throat met my chest hanging there, suspended and uncertain. But I was okay. My existence was becoming more commonplace as the morning progressed and last night's experience seeped out through the pores and cracks in my life. Yet I had been filled to such levels that even in this decline, I was more at peace than I could ever remember.

Memories tugged at me. As I watched them touch, I could feel the caress of Ellen's hands, the feel of her waist, her face. I longed for her with every cell in my body, but it was a tender desire that no longer hurt. Grief was cleanly absent. Somewhere deep inside, Ellen answered this longing, and I smiled.

I would miss Ellen for the rest of my life, but that terrible hole that she had left was filled.

I had discovered something quite surprising as the day awoke; *Ellen was not gone*, not nearly. She lived on. Not to say that she lived in memory, as others who have lost might express. That wasn't it at all; no, she was alive in actuality, breathing, feeling, touching the world from inside me.

It sounded crazy, and I wouldn't care to explain this to another soul, but I could feel her included nature. We were continuing our relationship. This was unexpected, and I had no idea what it would come to mean. But I caught a glimmer that I wasn't, in actuality, an individual, not the singular soul I had always imagined. I was wide and deep, a composite of so many standing in infinite beside me.

And today I noted occasional Ellen responses slide from me as my own. I was still the conceited, excited, and independent me, make no mistake, but I was me *and*.

"Oh God," the young woman was saying. "We shouldn't have come. I knew we shouldn't have come. What are we going to do now?" She broke her embrace and put her palms on the roof of the buried car. "I knew something bad was going to happen."

Did something bad happen? I was eavesdropping harmlessly from a few feet away. Okay, to be fair, I could understand it from her perspective. But it didn't feel that way to me. Something wonderful had happened, was happening. That's how it felt. I didn't know why the events were unfolding the way they were. It didn't matter. I trusted them.

"Damn it," said the young man as he looked at the visible half of their Datsun, obviously assessing the situation from a new level. Now that life was no longer in peril, the practicality of material loss and the reality of their predicament were settling in. On top of that, he also looked like he was in the doghouse.

"I have to be back the day after tomorrow!" Her face flashed with anger as she turned back around. She set on her boyfriend. "You know that. That was the whole idea!"

The heat had blossomed fully in the cove. The sand of the sliced-in-two beach was drying quickly and beginning to reflect the temperature back into my face. Having been here for many days, I knew what to expect. I had taken to spending my time hiding from the midday's heat either in the water or in the trailer with a 12-volt electric fan blowing on my face. I looked up at the craggy, rock-strewn slopes that led sharply out of the cove. Hugging their surface were remnants of the storm's mist, which were quickly being zapped away by the sun.

A few mornings back I had woken up early and climbed the canyon wall, picking around cat claws, other nastily thorned plants, and cactus of every description, sending loose rock down the aggressively steep hill as I labored. I had hoped to survey my surroundings and perhaps the adjoining coves that day. I turned back before 20 minutes had elapsed— before it was even 7 a.m.—because of the heat.

I sighed as I looked down at the miserable job of digging that lay ahead of the three of us. I really wasn't in the mood for miserable just now and, in my mind, told the car so.

Pop out of there, I told the car. Just pop on out of there on your own. Come on then.

I paused. That had sounded like Ellen.

The boy derailed my train of thought. "Can I use your shovel? This is a *goddamn* mess, I can tell you."

I looked down and realized I was leaning on my shovel like a prop. I was reluctant to give it up. "Hmmm," I said.

The young man took this to mean that further explanation was required.

"See, I've basically got to get the car functional by tonight. I'm going to have to clear all the sand from the outside. Who knows what I'm going to find when I lift the hood. I'm not much of a mechanic. What if I can't fix it? And I still have to figure out how I'm going to get it out of this hole after that. It has front-wheel drive with fair traction, but there's no way in hell I'll be able to drive it out."

He was processing intellectual goosh at light speed. His eyes stabbed at me. "Thank God you're here; I really need your help."

Hold on, slow down, wait a minute, I thought as I tried to chase the thread I had lost a moment ago. The boy's ambush of logic made me immediately weary. I couldn't stand it. That list felt terrible. What was it that I had been thinking that felt infinitely better?

Oh, yes, that was it. Come on, car. Pop up. Pop on out of there.

All of a sudden I had the strongest feeling. It almost made my feet start walking without instruction. I handed the lad the shovel and told him, "Just clear the center of the back bumper. No more. I've got an idea."

He reached out slowly to take the shovel.

"We're not going to work that hard," I said in the way of explanation. Then I left to wander into the desert foliage and trash that began at the back edge of the beach. He hopped down the crumbling ravine and began to dig. The girl watched me, perplexed.

I was hunting for something. It would have to be really stout and long. The chances of finding such an item seemed impossible to me, but then again, there had been that feeling. I was compelled to follow it. There was driftwood among the trash, even the pieces of an old rowboat. None of that would do.

This was an amazing mess back here. How could anyone trash a beautiful cove like this? Food wrappers and milk cartons printed unintelligibly in Spanish were thrown about. Disposable diapers, sun-bleached, wadded, their contents mummified, lay around in disgusting quantities. *Good Lord*, I thought.

Huge ant mounds protruded between the elephant bushes and barrel cactus. The ant homes incorporated trash into their very structure. I breathed tentatively as my nose picked up a septic smell. Toilet paper was everywhere. There was bigger stuff, too: canvas from tents, a few tent poles, broken containers, and boxes.

And then, in the midst of the garbage, there lay what I was searching for—the remnants of a boat-trailer frame. Everything of use had been stripped from it; wheels, axle, hitch, everything but the few pieces of I-beam that gave the trailer its overall shape, leaving essentially what was perfect for my needs.

This wasn't some RV'ers small boat trailer; it was a heavy unit 25 feet long, used to launch the skiffs of the local fishermen. The reason for its abandon was also clear. Its outer frame pieces had finally succumbed to the salted environment of ocean air. It was rusted through and had separated in a manner that could no longer be mended by welding, especially given the condition of the metal. Looking at this object and its improbable existence 50 yards from where I needed it, I should have been amazed. But I wasn't, not today.

Instead, I thought, *of course,* as I chuckled quietly to myself. I manhandled the main piece of the frame, hauling it toward the beach. The young lady ran up to lend a hand. Together we dragged, pushed, and cursed it to the cove as the sun broiled us.

"Thanks. Couldn't have done that without you." I wiped my rust-stained hands on the sand.

She smiled brightly.

"You got to be kidding," she said. "It's us who couldn't do without you."

I was embarrassed.

"I didn't have anything else going on," I answered, offering a poor attempt at wit.

"Yeah, right," she said.

"My pleasure," I said, correcting myself.

"Thank you." She squeezed my arm. Just then it meant the world to me that I had the opportunity to help.

We both sat, sweating profusely, as the boy crawled up out of the ditch looking much the same.

"This is miserable," he said.

"Granted," I replied. I looked down to see what had been accomplished. Only a fraction of the sand had been removed from the rear of the Datsun, but enough to expose the bumper. It was incredible how slow the progress had been.

"Sure you have to head back tomorrow?" I asked.

She cringed. It was a tormented clenching motion. There seemed to be more at work in her than this predicament on the beach.

The morning just kept getting hotter. This was compounded by moisture that was evaporating from yesterday's storm, making the desert air humid as well. I stood on the side of the narrow sand ravine and surveyed the damage.

The ravine was at its deepest where the Datsun, with its nose pointing out to sea, was half-buried in sand. Up at the mouth of the cove, where the natural canyon entered the beach, the terrain was much the same as it had been before the storm. The cut began there, gradually deepening across the beach through the car, until it met the surf of the ocean.

"Okay." I looked at the young man's strong frame. "We've got to get this I-beam to span the ravine just above and behind the car where you dug out the bumper. And"— I motioned to the young lady—"we need something to spread its weight so it won't dig into the sand. There was some driftwood and old boat pieces back in the trash that might do the trick."

She walked off into the bushes without a word. Whatever it was that was weighing on her was coming on stronger; you could see it in her walk.

The boy's strength was impressive. His muscles working under his shirt were definitely not just for show. He lifted the massive weight of the boat frame until it towered straight up 14 feet in the air. I helped him, but truly he supplied most of the work. The two of us let the frame fall like felled timber. It slammed heavily onto the ravine's opposite side, slicing into the sand and causing a small avalanche to pour down the slope and onto the car below. Fortunately, the area recently cleared around the bumper stayed cleared.

"Time for my secret weapon." I grinned. "Help her get something under the ends of this beam or we'll be wasting our time. I mean something with a lot of surface area, the size of a door or something, got it?"

He was becoming enthusiastic with action. "Got it!" he replied. I liked this kid.

The Land Cruiser's engine came to life, and its powerful idle filled me with that old sense of pride. This engine wasn't the original six-cylinder wimp the Japanese had installed for fuel economy. I had replaced that one with a large Chevy eight with 420 horses and several special improvements, something worthy of the rest of the Land Cruiser's engineering. This was an honest off-road vehicle, not some pansy Santa Fe four-wheel-drive used for taking kids to soccer. This vehicle had saved my ass more than once, and Ellen and I had broken and repaired it many times in our off-road adventures.

I maneuvered the vehicle to the top of the ravine and then drove down into to it. I stopped a few feet from the back bumper of the buried Datsun, left the engine going, opened the door and walked to the Land Cruiser's front bumper. There, on the bumper, mounted directly to the frame and wrapped completely in black vinyl with bungee cords, was the crown jewel of my off-road equipment: a 15-horse electric winch.

"Damn, that's beautiful." The boy appeared behind me. I beamed. I *really* liked this kid.

I climbed onto my hood and inspected the work the kids had done. Under either side of the I-beam there were now lengths of wood from the broken boat and several pieces of driftwood. I hoped it would do. I jumped down and unwound the steel cable from the winch and tossed it over the I-beam.

As soon as the cable landed in front of the buried Datsun, the young woman ran off into the dump once again. The boy and I peeked out of the ravine, watching curiously. She returned with a heavy canvas remnant from some tent, which she was folding as she walked back toward us.

When she reached the beam, she stepped out onto it like a gymnast, her young figure graceful as she leaned down to slide the canvas under the steel cable. Obviously, this was intended to protect the steel cable from the rough and rusted surface of the beam.

Clever girl, I thought and smiled appreciatively at her. Her return smile was now forced and distracted. The boy looped the steel cable around the frame of his Datsun and hooked it back on itself securely.

They catch on, I mused.

"Now clear off, you two. Get out of the ditch, I mean all the way out." They did so, quickly. There was some danger in what I was about to attempt.

I leaned lazily against the hood of my vehicle and began to summon that feeling I had had, the one that started this enterprise. I reached down to the controls on the side of the winch as if in a dream and slipped the motor into action.

Slowly the cable tightened, and at the same time, my chest felt as if it were floating up like a cork surfacing on water. The beam above me strained into its improvised supports on either side of the ravine. Small avalanches of white sand poured steadily down where it engaged the ledge. The winch worked harder and harder and nothing moved. The mechanical tension built in the cable. I grew lighter as I only half-watched.

Come on, come on. The iron-beam began to deflect and dish under the growing tons of pressure. A slow creaking groan grew from the mounting pressure of the metal cable, like the sound of a massive iron door opening wickedly on complaining hinges. And still the strain increased. If the cable broke and whiplashed at this tension, it would be deadly, likely cutting me in half on its way through the hood of the Land Cruiser. I involuntarily stepped to one side.

The force in the steel mounted. The heat from the sun poured into the ravine. The groan from the metal grew louder, demanding. The steel cable was now humming, and the beam bent dangerously. I was oblivious, elsewhere, following that feeling, expressing it, knowing it. *That's it, come on, hah!*

With a deep suction sound, the wet sand relinquished the Datsun. The back of the car popped up, just popped up, and the sand from the side of the banks fell into the hole that the rear wheels had vacated. The cable from the winch continued to work, lifting the rear bumper higher into the air.

My heart exploded.

Wow!

I quickly reached down to idle the winch.

Wow!

Everything stood still as I looked at the magic creation of the freed car. I was beginning to understand.

The young woman squealed in delight from up above and was jumping up and down.

"Yeah." The boy slapped his thigh in a manly outburst.

They observed that it was the winch that had turned the tide of these events, but I knew better.

Signs

"**N**o, oh no!" The young woman, who had been cheery for most of the arduous but hopeful afternoon, now looked as if she had just been harpooned. I only half-registered her response as I looked past and through her to the scene below. Finally, her utterances pierced my own astonishment, and I gazed at her. She stood sideways, centered in my view.

"Of course." She crossed her arms under her breasts and lifted a hand to her mouth. "What else?"

Her eyes were squeezed to thin slits under the blinding bright sun as she stood looking down from the slight rise at the canyon's top that overlooked the desert agricultural project. She gave a short hysterical laugh that mutated into a moan.

"Damn you!" she whispered to the scene. I switched my focus to her companion, who was obviously too stunned to respond to her.

Nothing had prepared any of us for what we were now seeing. It was surreal to the extreme, impossible, and I could only surmise that we were once again trapped.

Earlier this morning, after the Datsun had been extracted from the sand, the remaining activities had flowed easily, all things considered. I disassembled, dried and reassembled several parts under the hood, a few of which the boy had said he recognized, like the distributor cap.

It wasn't that long before I jumped the battery, and the car came sputtering to life after the third try.

However, even from the cove it was obvious the road through the canyon had been obliterated by last night's flash flood. There was no choice but for the Land Cruiser to tow the Datsun out. That seemed straightforward enough in principle, but in practice it took hours, since the passage had to be bolstered with rocks and sand in many places to get the lower-clearance car through.

The progress was continuous, although slow, and the young lady's spirits rose steadily because it was looking like things might work out after all. She talked of whizzing home to Arizona on the Mexican highway once they cleared the canyon, returning in time, perhaps a little later than planned but still in time.

I had resisted asking her about her need to get back. I knew she was worrying needlessly. But she hadn't offered any information, and she seemed reluctant to speak of what stressed her so.

Now, from our overlook, it was clear that her intentions of flight were impotent against the forces in the desert that summoned her to stay.

Below us, the acres of dry cotton plants were gone. The roads crisscrossing the fields were also gone. The houses and sheds scattered across the huge farming establishment weren't entirely visible. A few mounds of higher ground stuck out like islands, but for the most part the entire bowl of the giant desert agricultural project below us had become a shallow, glimmering lake.

I sat on a large rock beside the truck, pondering, trying to make sense of this new offering. I knew that immense quantities of water had poured out of last night's gale, more than I had ever experienced in my life. Everything about the beach this morning and the canyon this afternoon was a testimonial to that.

Still, this wasn't credible. I would have never thought so much water could be standing in the Sonoran Desert, not in my wildest imaginings. I studied the terrain below for passage or movement, anything that would signify that there was some connection to the highway 17 miles away, any connection other than by raft.

"Welcome to the Twilight Zone," I announced, crushing the hopes of my young wards.

I went to the Land Cruiser and returned to the rock, continuing my inspection with a pair of field binoculars. I noted that vehicles in the farm community had their topsides exposed to varying degrees, giving me an idea of the depth of water. It wasn't as bad as it first looked, but bad enough. I swept the binoculars in a systematic pattern, forcing myself to concentrate and look at every section of the sweep.

"I'm going to climb up this rise for a better look." The boy took off on his self-appointed mission.

I looked at my remaining companion, who was studying the scene with great intensity. I handed the girl the binoculars and told her to focus on the area I had been viewing. It took a moment or two; her scanning was less systematic, but I knew she caught the full impact of the view when she let out a gasp.

"We may be returning to the beach for a while," I said as I turned to walk to the Cruiser.

"No!" Her jaw was locked and she had tears in her eyes.

"A few days at most," I said, turning back to her. "It can keep."

From her expression I could see that it couldn't. I went back to sit with her. After collecting herself, she spoke.

"I'm pregnant," she hissed between her teeth in a hushed whisper. She sneaked a look up the rise to make sure the boy was out of earshot. My heart leaped.

"I put the appointment off to the last possible moment," she explained. "If I don't get back tomorrow, it'll be too late!"

The lad wasn't anywhere in sight. He had chosen the perfect time to leave.

"He doesn't know?"

"He doesn't know!"

"Yet you're telling me," I said. "Why me?"

That stumped her. She was trembling.

"That's okay," I said, half to myself. "I think I know why you're telling me."

She suddenly burst out with release. "It's a disaster!" Her voice was on the edge. "We *are* getting married. See? That's not it."

She turned her left hand to show a cute little diamond in white gold on the ring finger.

"Years from now, we'll have a family, but not now, at least not until after college. We're barely making it. We have so much debt. We can't leave college, because we've made huge commitments. How could we possibly pay off our student loans without careers?"

She glanced up the hill to where her fiancé had gone. "More than anything else, this accident would ruin his dreams, his future. I simply won't do that."

Heat radiated from the rocks and soil around us. The sun exposed every millimeter with burning light, pounded us, leaving no shadows anywhere. In the open without shade or shelter, the situation was becoming searing. Yet we were so preoccupied that neither of us acknowledged the intense pressure from our surroundings.

Thank God for sunscreen.

She continued talking, "We'll just have to find a way to get to that highway. I don't care if I have to swim. We *will* find a way ..." Her voice trailed off with finality, with ruinous conviction.

So, here it was. He had asked me to save him. But what could I do? There's no way to change someone's mind—guilt, force maybe, if you have the leverage, that might change their actions. None of that was for me.

I started questioning: could everything I'd lived change and be taken from me now? I'm sorry; I don't see where I have the power to influence this. I'd never been consulted.

To my surprise, even though she'd finished expressing her resolve, she kept talking.

"I'm early in the pregnancy. It's not more than a few cells. As long as I do it tomorrow, it's acceptable, and this will solve everything. We can always have children later. It's not an end-of-the-world decision."

Who was she trying to convince?

She was just a kid. I knew what it felt like, the future uncertain, and overwhelming disappointment left from previous generations roamed the earth to entangle her. She didn't yet know it was possible to sacrifice something and, at the same time, not give something up.

I stared at the glistening barrier lake that last night's storm had created. I began to think about my role. Perhaps I just needed to discover what she was asking.

After a while, I said, "Some not very small obstacles seem to be piling up here to slow down your decision."

She hugged herself around her belly. Her body language was obvious. She was telling me—no, her body was screaming it.

She was holding her womb.

Gad, I'm slow on the uptake. This is so simple.

Ellen, I thought silently to my soul mate, I'm compassionately dense; but I can learn if you hit me over the head hard enough. This younger woman *had* consulted me after all.

"What do *you* want?" I probed her.

She didn't answer, just held her belly tighter and started rocking. She was rocking her child.

I took her gently and forced her to face me.

"What do you really want?" I pressed her. Her eyes widened, looking at me, mouth working silently.

"It's okay," I whispered. "I'll agree. We'll work things out, find a way. Just say what you really want."

"I want our baby!" Her tears burst out, like last night's storm. She dived into my chest and wailed. I comforted her for the longest time.

Fortunately for me, she couldn't see the moist lines running on my cheeks. This was unbelievable, that I could hold her, hold them both. As I comforted her, I deftly dried my face on my shirt to hide the evidence.

After a while, I spoke. "You're gonna love this child; it's very special."

She stopped and looked up at me after I said that. I smiled.

Her tears were subsiding.

"I was going to take care of it quietly. No one was ever going to know." Once again, she looked up the hill toward her fiancé. "I know him. He'll quit school ... without even asking me. He's too smart and talented to work road construction or something. I couldn't stand the guilt."

I peered out over the lake.

"I don't think so. There are things in the universe that have a way of helping us out. Look at what this little storm is doing for you." I pointed to the water that trapped us. "There are angels out here for you in surprising forms."

"My God." She was wiping her eyes with the back of her bent hands, "I needed to hear this."

She shaded her eyes with her right hand and looked at the devastated fields, scanning for quite some time. Finally, she turned to me. She looked at me hard, and as I watched, a giant burden slipped from her handsome shoulders.

She breathed the words "Thank you."

It was a surprise when the filthy red quad-cab Ford pickup truck jumped up in front of us from the road's edge. Well, maybe not such a surprise after everything else. However, it was startling enough that I had to snatch the binoculars from the air like a pro receiver as they flew from her lap.

I looked up from my binoculars to the Mexican civilian getting out of the cab. The man looked like a cowboy; he wore crisp new Levi jeans that accented a shimmering silver Concho belt and a bright plaid long-sleeved shirt. It was my friend, my guardian angel from the road out of Hermosillo. The boy was shouting and waving hurrahs as he scrambled down the slope behind us.

As I watched, I became fascinated by how many people climbed out of the Mexican's quad cab. By the time he had walked over to me, there were six of them. He was chuckling.

"Well, well, what a surprise," he said. "I have been intending to come and check on you at the cove for weeks now, but work here has been demanding, *que no*." He was smiling broadly.

"But then, after the hurricane, well, we were headed there now to make sure you hadn't been washed away."

He was shaking my hand up and down.

Hurricane? That was a hurricane? There aren't hurricanes in the Gulf of California, are there? I looked down the slope at the Sonoran Desert farming project drowned under an impossible lake. Okay, maybe I was going to have to correct my thinking.

The six of them gathered to form a smiling line in front of us. Three were young men, two more gray-haired, and the sixth was a *señora*. In contrast with the cowboy Mexican, they were dressed shabbily in hard-working, dingy, and extremely muddy clothes.

"We never had proper introductions," he said. "I am Juan Carlos Juro. I am the engineer for this Campo Barcelonet farming project." He gestured expansively with his arm at the lake below us. "But right now most of my 1,000 hectares are under water."

I introduced myself and my two companions and explained I was towing them to the highway, or until now thought I was.

"That will be difficult," he said.

"I can see that."

"No, I don't think you can." He leaned back on one leg and was taking his cowboy hat off. "That is no problem." He was gesturing again at the lake. "It is next to the highway where the real problem is."

He wiped his forehead with the back of his cotton shirt and replaced his hat. The other six were having their own conversation in Spanish, quite oblivious to the chat Juan Carlos and I were having, leading me to believe that none of them spoke a word of English. They seemed to be admiring my Land Cruiser, or was I just proud?

"What are the conditions in the cove? It might be easier to go back there for four or five days and wait things out."

At his words, the young lady at my side shrugged and slipped her hand into her boyfriend's. From that, I knew it was no longer necessary for the young couple to stay. They should return.

"But you made it across," I said.

Juan Carlos eyed me, and then clucked his tongue.

"*Ay yi, yi.*" He looked down, then to the boy, then to me. "*Ay yi,*" he repeated. He turned and had a long conversation with his companions in musical Spanish. I'm going to learn Spanish, I promised myself for the hundredth time.

One of the young men left us and went into the cab, where we could see him pick up the microphone of the truck's CB radio. Juan Carlos sat on a rock ledge next to me, taking his hat off again. We all sat.

"Okay," he said. "We can give it a try. I was going to wait a day or two to venture to the other side of the project, but my wife is anxious to see me as well."

The No Road Out

We followed Juan Carlos's tall quad-cab truck as it picked its way down the rise. The Datsun was next, and I followed last in the mighty blue Land Cruiser. When the pickup stopped at the edge of the temporary lake, its occupants swarmed out once again.

I remembered that the agricultural plots were laid out in large square grids bordered on all four sides with dusty dirt roads. But now all the roads, along with the fields, were gone, covered by a sheet of reflecting water.

We needed a boat.

I tried to estimate where the road lay under the water from various indicators poking out of the water. I could see the tops of some ruined cotton plants defining higher areas that had once been fields. Also, I observed scattered huts and houses that must lay slightly off the submerged roads. These structures were in water as high as a foot below their window seals. Then far to our right, I saw the termination of the run of power lines. The power poles marched away toward somewhere north where the highway must eventually be. They formed a zigzag sequence of right angles.

Juan Carlos was sizing up our vehicles. As he leaned down on one knee, inspecting the back of my Land Cruiser, his eyes grew wide. He looked up, as if seeing me for the first time, then looked back to my plates and back to me.

Just then, his crew and the kids rounded the front of the Land Cruiser and headed toward us. Juan Carlos quickly reached into the lakeshore muck and, grabbing a handful of wet mud, smeared it over the right lower corner of my license plate, hiding the incriminating markings.

"Of course, the green car will not be driving this part," he said simply without skipping a beat. He stood, wiping a muddy hand on clean blue jeans and eyed me secretively, but with ferocity. He pointed to the kids. "They'll ride with you, okay?"

Next he instructed his crew and they went to backing up his high-clearance pickup and started tying towlines to it.

Juan Carlos watched them silently, lost in some internal struggle. I was shocked by his discretion. Not for the first time, I sensed he might be more than he appeared.

"Now," he said, looking off at the line of power poles, "you can't stop, do you understand? If you stop, you will not go again. The mud will have you."

I couldn't believe we were about to drive through a lake.

"That water will swamp my intake and drown my engine," I said.

"Yes, perhaps," agreed Juan Carlos. "Your Toyota's engine is a bit lower to the ground than mine. This morning I thought it would be a problem in my truck, but I have been doing this a lot today, and so have several of our vehicles, some lower than yours. We have had many rescues, you see." He beamed at me. "You have to go fast enough so the water does not have time to fall back in, like plowing snow in front of a fast-moving blade. That's for the straightaway, but at the corner of every field, you will have to turn. If you turn too slow, you will be stuck; if you turn too fast, you'll slide and be trapped in the field." He paused then, thinking what to add. "You'll figure it out."

Not much comfort.

"You must follow me exactly and keep up, okay?"

Oh, boy, I thought, and turned to the kids. Both of their jaws were hanging open.

"Not too late to change your mind," I said. "Want to go back to the beach?"

"Hell yes," said the lad.

"Hell no!" said the lass, kneeing him in the thigh. I enjoyed her spunk, not for the last time. I watched as she scampered into the front seat of my truck, relegating the boy to the back seat.

Juan Carlos's crew swarmed back into his quad cab, leaving him and me alone for a moment. The expression on his face changed.

"You've guessed what's going on here?" I asked.

He nodded.

"You're taking it rather well."

Juan Carlos took his hat from his head and, with fully

opened eyes, looked directly into the burning sun.

"Even weeks ago, when we met on the highway," he said, "I sensed it. But still you've surprised me."

I didn't know what to say. The mystery that I awoke to this morning, with those young kids, was mind-boggling, to be sure. But after Ellen's appearance, it simply fell into place. However, Juan Carlos was unexpected. In the afterglow of last night's journey, I remained a smidgen outside the world as well as within it. From that perspective, nothing seemed entirely real.

I looked at Juan Carlos again. It was then I noticed his hatband, which was not a hatband at all but a *japa mala*—Hindu prayer beads and, judging by their appearance, very old. Here, in what was surely a rigid and traditional Chihuahua archdiocese, those couldn't be more out of place.

"You're not really the engineer for Campo Barcelonet, are you?" I asked.

"Of course I am," was his reply. His brown eyes, under thick black eyebrows, bored into me. Then Juan Carlos made a sweeping gesture across the valley with his hat. "These are my people. I come from them. As the engineer, I watch over them, but also in another way. I am Na'wal."

I shrugged. It was obvious that that held no meaning for me.

"The simple rural *españoles* regard Na'wal as a witch, or *brujo*. But that is the *superstición* of narrow minds, of those that do not comprehend."

Juan Carlos's words fell off as he stared at the water-changed landscape.

"For the ancient Toltec, Na'wal were holy ones," he explained. "Their practices and spiritual knowledge have been concealed but passed down for millennia. I was educated by my uncle's lineage—I walk the path of a man of knowledge." Juan Carlos smiled slightly, letting me consider that. Then he added, "Perhaps I should not entirely surprise you."

Something inside me wasn't ready for this conversation.

So I looked over at the Land Cruiser. The girl was talking intensely to the new father inside the cab. His face was stricken, and the atmosphere looked thick. The kids were obviously too busy to wonder what was detaining us.

"How can they be here?" I questioned absently.

Juan Carlos looked at them with narrowing eyes. Then he looked at me.

"*They?* They are where they belong. It is you, my friend, that is not."

Me?

The landscape winked and for an instant swam in front of me. Everything suddenly snapped into place. I wasn't even shocked. In fact, the day tasted sweeter. I smiled. In my mind, I traced every moment of the last weeks; and they all traced forward in time to now. Somewhere, I'd missed a step. Eventually, he asked, "So the real question, David, is how you've come to be here?"

"I don't know."

His question echoed in my mind, reverberating with memories of the existence I'd known only weeks ago—a lifetime ago—a cottony existence from before all had been taken from me in a violent car crash a thousand feet from my home, from before those moments in a near-vertical chute of red stone where my heart had stopped pumping blood—for several minutes.

In that prior life, I numbly recalled, I'd been a seeker. Now I was nothing. I had sought something extraordinary—to live from source, the magic life. My lips pronounced this out loud even as my mind wrestled it down.

Juan Carlos, listening to more than I said, turned toward me. "We'll not share this time together for long, you and I. But I can tell you, no one finds what you seek until they are ready to lose themselves."

He left me standing there. I watched him return to his truck, a brown man of sparse words, words that I obviously wasn't meant to ponder just then, because I barely had time to jump into the Land Cruiser's driver seat and crank up the engine before Juan Carlos met the water at high speed with the Datsun in tow. The kids in my truck held hands between the seats in silence.

His rig troweled the water, sending up plumes 3 feet high and 15 feet long to either side, creating a trough through which the two vehicles rode, and the water fell back neatly together behind the Datsun.

I offered a fictional toast—"Here's to bizarre"—and hit it.

It wasn't so bad once you learned to ignore the panicky sensation that the water ahead might become an actual lake, one that would deepen and swallow your vehicle, where imagination suggested you would plummet to submerged depths and have to make one of those Hollywood kick-out-the-window-and-swim-up escapes. Aside from that, it wasn't too bad.

Actually, the water level varied quite a bit, sometimes as low as the front bumper and most of the time staying below the top of the radiator. The pluming water was propelled away such that not much seeped through the floor seams at the bottom of the doors.

As we passed, I could see places where workers toiled with salvage operations up to their knees in water and muck. Other places, where nothing protruded, looked quite deep. We were coming up to the first irrigation cistern, and the hurricane's deposited water was only halfway up its outer wall. Its electric hut was high and dry. The pipe was still thundering water into the cistern, which pumped additional unneeded water into the ruined fields. The cistern was on the left side, meaning the road would turn there.

I kept focused on the red quad-cab and Datsun that sped through the water, leading the way.

The water was shallower at this first left turn, so even though I lost the plowing action as I slowed, it turned out not to be a problem. That was also true for the first right and second left turns.

It was the second right turn that got me. On the approach,

I could see a flow of ripples in the water on the far side of the turn. It looked strangely like a river flowing in a lake. The water stayed deep this time, and as I slowed to turn, it fell around the vehicle almost as high as the door handles.

Perhaps I took the turn too fast, for the next thing I knew, the Land Cruiser was skidding sideways. Counter-steering was useless in this much water as we careened directly into the current of that surreal river that crossed the lake. As I fought for control, I couldn't believe Juan Carlos had made it. Then I realized it was probably his passage that caused the underwater slick that had caught me.

As we came to rest, the water swept over the hood began flowing through the seams under the doors, and the engine stopped, but Juan Carlos didn't. The three of us watched as he plumed away, left, right, then out of sight.

There was obviously no point in trying to restart the drowned engine. I looked disgustedly as the water formed a pool on the floorboard below the accelerator.

"Now what?" I uttered. I wasn't referring to this present jam. I already knew its outcome.

For a time we just sat looking out at the water that imprisoned our vehicle in all directions. The two kids looked horrified. We were trapped, and I nearly made a critical mistake. I hurriedly pressed switches and was relieved to see that the electric was still working enough to roll down the windows, or at least three of them before shorting out somewhere in the chassis.

I told the kids to wiggle out onto the roof, to get a look and see if they could tell the whereabouts of Juan Carlos. Presently, they informed me they saw him driving out of the water onto higher ground near some huge structures. Next they reported that Juan Carlos had gotten out and was giving us thumbs up from the hood of his truck. I translated the sign language for the kids by explaining it meant we were in for a wait. They wisely elected to stay aloft after looking back down inside the vehicle.

Now that we had come to a rest, the water no longer swept over the hood, though it wasn't much lower than that surface. The seeping of water into the Land Cruiser's interior was slow but steady, and I knew it would eventually go beyond the level of my seat and force me out.

Amazingly, the view of the interior's ruination didn't bother me. I sat in the mighty blue Land Cruiser saying goodbye to it, and as I said goodbye, I closed the book on my past.

The road had vanished, and I was about to have no vehicle.

Alone in the driver seat, I reconsidered my question. "Now what?"

No Road, No Vehicle

Yellow Signs are suggestions
White signs are rules masquerading as laws
True laws cannot be broken

It is hard to tell the difference

Water was everywhere, beautiful, sparkling, unwanted; mocking the desert sun, and by now as high as my shins inside the Land Cruiser. It was sweeping over the hood of my vehicle cocoon.

The sun fought furiously to evaporate the change that had descended on the Sonoran sand, but to no avail. The desert's hardpan surface was struggling to channel water elsewhere, shed it, or at least spread it out, to where its power would diminish.

However, this change had come with work to do and would not leave without having done it. So, there was water everywhere that didn't seem to fit, or be appropriate in a desert. This incongruity couldn't be accounted for and had effects that couldn't be estimated, except that, in the end it was bound to swell and explode the sheath of the hardened desert shell. There was no telling what might emerge from the tender underbelly of the thick-skinned desert.

Was this predicament by chance or inevitable? At the moment, I couldn't see the difference. If there's a chance for something, given enough time, it's inevitable.

No Vehicle, No Road. "So now what?"

I'd entered the realm of limbo, no longer condemned to the eternal suffering I'd experienced since Ellen's death, yet still barred from entry into heaven. I knew, too well, why I was set on this path; and upon it, the fundamental but inconceivable had occurred. So I'd been only mildly surprised by the appearance of a Juan Carlos. But his words shook me.

To find what I seek, I must first lose myself.

I held no delusion about what he was suggesting. Every road I'd ventured, won, suffered, or lost myself on led to this.

What I seek is true magic in life, and I've crashed headlong into *me*.

I am the wall.

And magic is not about walking through walls—or swimming in soil, creating red trucks or houses, remote viewing, psychic healing, or going around man's physical illusion. Perhaps all that's available, but what difference does it make if the heart is misaligned?

Why is my heart askew?

The answer begins in stepping outside *me*—losing myself. Juan Carlos pointed the way.

The water continually filled the Land Cruiser's interior. I stirred the muddy mess with my ankles.

I couldn't account for the incongruities in the last three

years of my life any more than I could account for them here as I sat in a bone-dry desert, up to my shins in swamp. However, in retrospect, I began to sense perfection.

By turning his back on me and our friendship, my business partner was able to begin healing his life. This would have been impossible while he felt responsible for my welfare. Were his actions selfish, coldhearted, betrayal? Or were they inspired emancipation? Both, and neither. I would no longer judge it. He'd found a way. At any rate, he'd demonstrated the damage I inflict from indifference and helped me learn the profound lesson of forgiveness.

The water was up another few inches now. Some ruined belongings floated below my knees, and more floated beneath the passenger seat at my right side. Over there, bobbing in the water, was a bulb of lip gloss that remained from Ellen's life. I reached and fished it out and held it. This had also known Ellen's lips.

For three years I had worked to reform my heart, to see Ellen as she was, love her strengths and her frailties; help free her from the chains forged by years of my criticism. Amazingly, as I improved, she grew angry. The more I amended my ways, the more volatile and outraged she became. Initially, I considered this to be ironic, except it wasn't funny.

I wondered how any couple could ever set right the procession of relationship mistakes cast in time's iron. I understood it, though. As I released the pressure on those compartments in her heart, and she allowed them to breathe air, the long-smothered hurt that had been smoldering there exploded with furious fire, for it could inhale at last. I tried to not be discouraged by her anger with me. I let the flames burn themselves out, one at a time, and made atonement.

The relationship fell short within me, but also within her. We'll fail each other. That's given. But I've brooded far too long over how others treat me and failed to notice it's how I treat them that fashions my happiness.

Ellen and I finally consummated our love for each other.

All these uninvited gifts had been hidden underneath painful wrappers, and I had no clue, except that I had asked for great things.

I plopped her lip gloss back into the rising water.

Then why should Ellen die?

But there's no answer to death. Death isn't even a question.

Even if we, who are left behind, comfort ourselves by speculating that it was the right time for someone, we can never know for sure. I liked to believe that parting is always perfect in time and by complete consent—even if the ego isn't in on it. At best, I hope to recognize my own end at all three levels and be at peace with it, as was Futzu.

This much *is* certain, though. Loved ones are left behind with every passing from the road, and the more one touches, the more there are left who grieve.

So for those of us left to journey alone, there's no sense to be made in the loss, except it makes perfect sense in the passing of life to next generations, from my father basket-maker to his daughter cliff-dweller, to children of settlers and from son of man.

The water was rising to my knees, urging, wanting to push me out. But I wasn't ready.

I did know, however, the uniqueness of the gift I had received. In that nonphysical moment, beyond breath and life, Ellen had reached out and shown me. The world isn't broken because hell exists here alongside heaven. That's by design. All dualities are intended, exquisitely balanced, and between their extremes lies choice. Pain exists so we can know joy. But we cannot *be* two things at once; and so, as I am free to choose, I will choose joy.

The water was now above the seat, entering my pockets.

I supposed this was sufficient. I'd never fully realize the true nature of things. I could probe them as deeply as possible with my senses, invent spiritual models and philosophize until the holy cows come home. None of that had ever proved more than could be seen, touched, or smelled. Not for me anyway, a common man. I'd confirmed, however, through profound attraction, the existence of a deeper function unseen, and that we commune with it in the abstract. Nonetheless, no matter how hard I peer at the dash of my car, I see only a dashboard—even if science and spirit tell me that its nature is otherwise.

That's what it means to be human in a supernatural world.

It wasn't my aim to unravel the mysteries. I was here to be part of them; besides, the ordinary *was* extraordinary.

I stared at the water rising into my lap as it readied to cast me out.

Was I prepared to surrender myself? Juan Carlos had asked.

Scary stuff!

What about me? Little I'd done in life strayed far from looking out for me; at the very least I've always included looking out for me. I'm sure that's normal. Most everyone acts in terms of safety or personal benefit. And we all need others to be a certain way. A dream of life built on bricks of self-preservation, mortared with fear, constructing walls to separate what we will love from what we will not, taking everything personally. This is the dwelling so commonplace that it feels proper.

But what if, instead, I knew I was cared for, my every desire assured by a solid contract. Then I could easily surrender myself to some greater purpose.

Futzu had told his students to polish their mirrors—*make your mind as a mirror polished a thousand times* ... until there remains no speck of doubt.

After all that's happened to me, what I've seen, the angels that have come to my aid, I had to say—there remained no doubt. I know I'm cared for.

Juan Carlos brought the question. And I was preparing an answer—*Yes*.

I knew such a decision changed nothing. "How many times?" asked the master.

But this would form my starting place, like the first day of quitting cigarettes. I would practice. All that had gone before left me prepared for this final chapter, which was about to become my first chapter.

I solicited the unseen for help, some easy step—what would you have me do?

A solid *thunk* sounded from the driver's door at my elbow. It startled me and then banged again. Out my window, in the current of the false river, which flowed through the false lake, was a true object banging against my door.

I stretched up, shedding some of the waist-deep water, to get a better look.

Outside my truck was a chest, made of ironwood—heavy. That shouldn't be able to float. I leaned my belly button on the door's ledge and reached for it. The current brought it to my hands. I splashed back down into the driver's seat with it in my lap. It was small. The lid and sides were ornately carved, and its craftsmanship suggested why it had been able to float. The air inside must have been sealed by the well-built, tight-fitting lid.

Would I tear into this wooden chest to inspect or possess its contents, as if a thing lost by another was my prize?

I didn't disturb its seal; this didn't belong to me. That realization was fresh, and I wasn't sure how I came to it. There was one thing this could mean. In my past, every angel that had appeared was of flesh and blood. Where do you think angels come from, after all?

I smiled.

So, all the while, it was simply the act of going that was of greatest importance—here is the map, there is the road and the signs upon it.

The water inside was now up to the level of the water outside. Taking the ironwood chest, I climbed out of the drowned Land Cruiser and onto the roof.

That's when I saw the monster approaching.

Angels

When waiting for a surplus to share from my plate
Never have I enough to spare
Upon sharing what little I have,
Ever is my plate in surplus

(transliterated on the morning of day two)

It drove toward us through the lake barely getting its monstrous toes wet. Black smoke belched out of its vertical snout. Its rear wheels towered in height three times taller than a man, though it was a man who sat in the cab operating it, looking dwarfed by the sheer size of the machine. Even at a distance, I could tell it was the biggest tractor I'd ever seen.

Three other minions of the tractor rode on it behind the cab, all bearing white teeth behind nut-brown faces. They spoke their alien language at us as the tractor swung around and backed up to position its three-point hitch above our hood. They jumped out into water above their waists and dived under to hook a chain to the Land Cruiser's tow hooks, which were submerged with the front bumper.

I can only imagine what it looked like to the observers on the shore as this giant tractor came from the lake pulling our vehicle, the size of a child's toy in contrast, with three wet dolls perched on the roof. It parted the waters and climbed up onto the shores of the Promised Land.

We had the wrong idea that our flood-capades were now behind us.

We got down off the roof to shake hands with Juan Carlos and saw the green Datsun parked out of the sun under a mammoth storage structure.

Juan Carlos noticed the water coming out the door seams of my vehicle and went to look inside. He pulled open the driver's door and water cascaded out of the interior.

The farm workers and villagers had a lunch waiting for us. The scene was completely out of place: bright-colored blankets spread on the ground with mangos, tortillas, bowls of *pico de gallo*, and *carne asada*, all against a backdrop of the hurricane's devastation. Behind the colorful lunch was the shore of knee-deep water, floating with debris around living quarters. Behind that lay more ruined fields. Tanned and sodden people were working in and around their homes trying to recover belongings, working to salvage their lives. This must have been living areas for most of those who worked on the project.

One of the men who had come to rescue us with the tractor walked over to the tablecloths and hugged a woman who had been helping with the meal. Together they walked into the muddy water. I watched as they waded to a nearby flooded house. The man went inside the open door and soon reappeared with a small box of sodden belongings. His *señora* looked stricken.

I was becoming incredibly self-conscious and embarrassed about how much so many were doing on our behalf. These people had set aside the tragedies of the hurricane to help us. Why? Our problems couldn't possibly be as urgent as the loss I witnessed them struggle against.

So appalled was I by the revelation that the woman at my side had to grab my shoulder. She continued to lavish me with Spanish. I looked then at the old woman, her face brown with folded wrinkles telling her years. She was no taller than my shoulder. Her beautiful smile and youthful blue eyes transcended age.

I sensed in the ancient woman the sparkling young lady she had been. Her skirt was adobe blue down to the knees, below which it was completely ruined by red sod. Her sandals were broken by hardening mud. Realizing I had no idea what she was saying, she took my elbow and gently led me to the colorful feast laid out on the ground and bade me sit down. I wondered if she'd eaten today.

I was humbled beyond belief. I realized I didn't know how to receive such a gift from another human soul. I didn't know how to accept so much, because I don't think I knew how to give like that.

I wanted to.

Do something, anything for these people! Anything.

Suddenly, I had a strong impulse.

Instead of sitting, as the old woman had urged, I held up a finger in the air and said, "*Un momento, señora, por favor.*"

She watched as I walked the short distance to my drowned vehicle.

I stood after reaching into the Land Cruiser, holding the ironwood chest. Having virtually no Spanish words, I held the chest above my head and whistled loudly.

I'd learned to whistle shrilly like that in grammar school. Very annoying, probably hadn't done it since I was a kid, but this was as effective a form of communication as any.

Dozens of brown eyes stopped what they were doing to look at me, those nearby, those in and around the open sheds behind me, and those in the knee-high water wandering the drowned homes. Juan Carlos, now with a pleasant-looking middle-aged woman on his arm, eyed me with humor. I held the chest higher, turning it in my hands to see if anyone would respond.

It was the old woman in the adobe blue skirt whose youthful eyes grew wide. Her hand came to her mouth.

My hunch paid off ... or was it a hunch?

I walked backed to the area of colorfully laid lunch, bent and presented the ironwood chest to the aged *señora*. She collapsed with it to the ground.

Words poured from her as she caressed the chest and cried. The only word I could pick out was "*Gracias.*" She hugged the chest and then reached for my hand. I sat next to her as she opened it. The child in her sang with delight when she found no water inside. Inside, instead, were old photos and beautiful items.

"It was her husband's." The voice came from the woman

who had been on Juan Carlos's arm, who I would later learn was Juan Carlos's wife. She and Juan Carlos were standing behind me.

Juan Carlos's wife said, "Her husband was an artisan and made many things we loved. I knew them both since I was a child. Her husband died and she has lived half her lifetime without him."

I sensed familiar signs woven in the landscape, like a silent lover pulling on my heart. This was an easy gift to give, since everything in the universe prepared to help me give it. The old woman carefully went through the contents and pulled out a silver chain. Upon it was an unusual piece of jewelry in the form of delicate silver wings, inlaid with splinters of agate and turquoise.

My jaw dropped in recognition. *He had wings.*

She leaned into me for what I thought would be an embrace; instead she pulled away having hung the chain around my neck.

At that moment, I fell in love with this wrinkled *señora.* Her tear-moistened hand touched mine, and she smiled with broken and crooked teeth.

I looked up and the desert just sparkled. Dusty storage structures with antique tractors, mounds of cactus, wandering farmworkers, and a shimmering lake were all bathed in story-book glow.

This is how I had experienced the world as a preschooler, every panorama dancing before me, playful and fun. The air was sweet, and I wanted to touch everything. What would I give to feel this every second? It had taken half a lifetime to discover that doing things for me never completely did it for me.

I fingered the silver wings the old woman gave me and smiled in thanks for such a gift.

"Never until now," remarked Juan Carlos's wife, "have I seen her open that box for another."

• • •

"I'm sorry to make you wait so long." Juan Carlos was leading us toward the structures where the Datsun was parked. "But the tractors were on the other side of the fields, and we will need them now. The highway is cut off."

At first I was puzzled by what he meant. Then he led us behind the structures to get a view north and to the highway.

There it was, the road restored unto us, like a promise, marching to the horizon. The highway looked grand, high and dry. It was the scene between us and the highway that made our hearts sink.

A wild, tumultuous river raged in the normally dry arroyo that paralleled the highway, with unbelievable rapids and speed. It was obviously deep, and as daring a white-water enthusiast as I've been, I wouldn't risk a raft in that watery thunder, let alone a vehicle.

We were cut off once again, for the third and last time.

Destinations

In beauty I walk
With beauty before me I walk
With beauty behind me I walk
With beauty above me I walk
With beauty around me I walk
It has become beauty again

(They walk in beauty. They are beautiful people.)

Di'neh (Navajo) beauty way prayer

The farmworkers lifted the front of the Datsun as high as possible with the three-point hitch of the behemoth tractor, so high that it dragged the rear bumper a bit. The idea was to keep the engine out of water so it could drive off on the highway once the torrent was crossed.

I was surprised by and thoroughly enjoyed the hug of thanks and goodbye from the lad, and I pooh-poohed his feelings of guilt about my drowned transportation.

"No problem. I'll dry her out and she'll be as good as new," I lied.

When the young lady gave me a hug, it was like all the hugs my Ellen had ever given me rolled into one, and therefore I couldn't let go.

She must have had her own reasons for lingering, because her embrace was long, sustained, and gently rocked me. I imagined the young infant in her womb and was grateful for this miraculous opportunity to play my part.

With a roar, the giant tractor coursed to life, belching diesel smoke out its stack, and they were leaving my life, off to continue their own. I was proud of this first step I had taken into a larger world, and those two terrific kids would never know how large and far-reaching those steps had been.

The tractor pulled their car into the rushing floodwater that formed the last barrier to the highway. For an alarming moment, the tractor started being swept downstream as the water plowed into its huge, 15-foot-diameter rear wheels. The idea that that mammoth tractor could be forced sideways was shocking. I was holding my breath, amazed at the spectacle. It fought forward, got purchase, swept a little more down current, and fought forward again. Finally it leaped out of the ditch with the Datsun in its wake.

We were now separated by a gulf as wide as the Baja's ocean, but I could see across it, observing them through time and space. The workers helped the young couple unhitch. I watched as David opened the driver-side door to start the engine. It puffed to life with a long cough of white smoke. And just like that, they were gone.

I'd always hated that green Datsun, I mused. I happened to know for certain it was going home to a junkyard. Ellen and I had bought it out of the paper from a large slovenly lady who met us in a dark grocery-store parking lot at night. So I guess I can claim I never got a good look at it until it was home. We spent 1,200 unrequited dollars. The Datsun was broken down and parked at the dorms most of the time, and otherwise we got just one trip out of it, this trip to Mexico; the trip that I'd never known until today had saved our first child's life.

"Well, David." Juan Carlos clapped me on the back "You'll come to my *casa* for supper. Stay here in this time with me and my *señora* for a while more, yes? We'll crack open your saga."

"You couldn't know how much that would mean to me, Juan Carlos." If desired, you can learn to recognize those from your soul group the instant you meet them on the road. It seemed we had a lot of catching up to do, even though we were strangers. I would love nothing more than to learn Juan Carlos's tale and tell him mine.

Well, maybe I'd have to leave a few parts out—I paused, considering the man who called himself Na'wal—or would I?

My heart was soaring, and magic was in the air. All the presents lay unwrapped around me. The universe had delivered more than I'd asked for. I could even now say with authority, "Don't be afraid of the oddly shaped packages."

I wasn't alone, never would be. I was with Ellen. I could see across time, and my heart was bursting. I wanted this feeling to last without end, and since this love was not of things, I prepared myself to gather all these gifts and share them with others from here forward.

I turned to close my vehicle's door for the last time and lingered with a hand on the door, saying goodbye to the mighty blue Land Cruiser, which had been Ellen's and mine.

I peered at my reflection in the driver's-side window. I hadn't looked at my unshaven face in weeks. That was the start of quite a beard and mustache. With a bit of grooming, that would look really good.

I smiled at my reflection.

A brilliantly strong and vibrant senior face smiled back at me from the Land Cruiser's reflecting glass. Perfect teeth sparkled behind a striking mustache and groomed gray beard, shiny baldness aloft. Eyes twinkled in our connected gaze. It didn't actually occur in the face muscles, but something in the reflection winked at me, and the eternal smile, which was not for me, increased just a tick. I sensed something kindred.

I felt warm.

11 And upon seeing that God had made vanish from the earth all the Road that was between places,

12 mankind took to the skies.